MY BEST MISTAKE

TASHA'S STORY

CAROLE WOLFE

BLIND VISTA PRESS

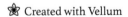 Created with Vellum

DEDICATION

To everyone who cheered me on over the years, I couldn't have done it without you!

1

Tasha crumpled the letter in her hand and threw it on the floor. Without thinking, she pushed a week's worth of mail from the coffee table and watched it scatter, burying the offending missive.

"How could he do this?" she asked the empty living room. Pressing the palms of her hands against her eye sockets, she forced herself to calm down. The new housecleaner was due any minute, and the place was so messy and cluttered, Tasha was sure the housecleaner would resign as soon as she walked in the door. Just like the last one did. And the one before that.

Why did she decide to open mail instead of tidy up?

"Because I didn't expect another threatening letter from my loser of an ex-husband."

She took a deep breath and pushed her overgrown bangs out of her eyes. She'd forgotten to make a hair appointment, and she didn't have time to make the call right now. Instead, Tasha leaned down to clean up her mess.

Tasha sorted the junk mail into one pile and anything that looked important, including the crumpled legal notice, into another. She shoved the discarded mail into a trash bag with a water bottle and empty chip container. Tasha picked up several pillows that lay on the floor and arranged them on the couch, before grabbing the stack of mail and heading for the kitchen.

She tossed the mail on the counter, took the trash outside, and then dashed back to the living room. She spun around to survey the damage. As usual, the place was a disaster. Tasha fought back tears as she grabbed the laundry basket partially full of clothes. She threw anything that didn't belong into the basket.

"How dare he?" Tasha muttered as she grabbed an action figure off the side table and pitched it into the basket. A coloring book followed, then a toy dump truck.

Just as she was ready to empty the overflowing basket, the doorbell rang. Tasha looked around the room.

"Oh crap. Where can I stash this?"

The bell rang again, and she dashed to the center of the room. Tasha shoved the laundry basket under the coffee table.

"Good enough."

Running back to the front door, Tasha flung open the door and greeted her visitor. A woman wearing a bright yellow T-shirt and khaki pants smiled at her. A vacuum cleaner and caddy of supplies sat on the ground next to her. A tool belt holding several sizes and shapes of feather dusters completed the woman's look.

"Hi, I'm Sunshine. I'm here to clean your house."

Hoping the woman would remain as cheery when she saw the inside of the house, Tasha invited her in. The woman hauled her supplies inside and took a look around. The housecleaner's eyes widened, but she didn't say anything. Praying her rushed efforts were enough, Tasha said, "I'll be in the kitchen if you need me."

Feeling like a failure for running away, Tasha hurried into the kitchen where another mess greeted her. Letting out a sigh, Tasha took the dirty breakfast dishes out of the sink and loaded the dishwasher before turning to the jumble of cereal boxes on the countertop. As she returned the food to the pantry, she thought about why she was so disorganized. *Picking up after yourself isn't that hard. Mom does it. Sara does it. Even my daughter does it.*

If she picked up after herself, she wouldn't have to worry about her house being a mess. She didn't want to look like a complete failure when someone visited. Tasha failed at enough as it was.

Shaking her head in disgust, she grabbed a rag from the sink and wiped down the countertops and the kitchen table.

"There is no way I'm going to let another housecleaner fire me again for being too messy." She remembered the lecture she got last month as she scrubbed at a dried-on spot of pancake batter. Tasha smiled when it came loose. "I can keep a clean house."

As she worked on a splatter of spaghetti sauce, her mind wandered back to the letter she'd crumpled. What could Doug be up to now? All he usually wanted was money. If she wrote him a check, he'd go away for a while.

Tasha bit her lip. What had she done with her checkbook? She needed it to pay the housecleaner. Dropping the rag, she grabbed her purse, and dumped out its contents. Lip gloss, paper scraps, and loose change covered the countertop, but no checkbook. Shoving everything back into her purse, she began searching through the kitchen drawers. She found it stuck under an expired coupon book and Libby's field trip form from last year. Throwing the book and form away, Tasha grabbed her checkbook.

Might as well pay Sunshine now, she thought and headed back to the living room. The housecleaner glanced up and Tasha froze. Sunshine wasn't very sunny.

"You undersold this job. The place is a mess," she said

crossing her arms over her chest. "I'll clean it, but I'll have to charge you double the quote."

Tasha nodded and waved her checkbook.

"Not a problem. I'll give you the check now, so I don't forget."

The housecleaner studied her. At first, she thought Sunshine was thrown off that she hadn't argued with the price change, but then Tasha saw *The Look*. It was the look of recognition strangers got when they realized who she was. Hoping to hide her face, Tasha glanced down, but it was too late.

Oh no. Here it comes.

"You seem familiar," the housecleaner said. "Have you been on the news or something?"

Tasha's face flushed as she filled out the check. She scribbled her signature, keeping her head down.

"Not for a couple of years."

"I knew it. You're famous, aren't you?"

"I've had my five minutes of fame." Tasha shook her head and handed over the check. "I don't recommend it. Not worth the trouble."

The woman looked down at the check.

"Natasha Gerome. That name rings a bell." Returning her gaze to her face, she asked, "Come on. You gotta tell me now. Who are you?"

Tasha sighed. Experience told her Sunshine wouldn't take no for an answer. She also knew after she told her, she would need a new housecleaner. It never failed: as soon as people found out how much money she had things got weird.

Hoping for the best, Tasha said, "I won the lottery about eight years ago. That's probably why I look familiar."

"Oh my God. You're the one whose husband freaked out on national TV about his twins not being his. He had an affair with your real estate agent." The woman's eyes grew as large as saucers. "My husband is never going to believe this."

At least she didn't mention the $116 million payday.

The doorbell rang before Tasha could speak. Grateful for the interruption, Tasha shrugged to Sunshine and turned to the door.

Please don't let this day get any worse, she thought as she yanked open the door. Her shoulders drooped when she saw who was there.

"This is not a good time."

"That's no way to greet your mother, sweetie," said Helene as she brushed past her daughter. "How are you today?"

2

Irritated by her mother's arrival, Tasha closed the door.

"I didn't know you were stopping by. To what do I owe this pleasure of a surprise visit?"

"A new cleaning service, sweetie?" her mother asked. In typical Helene-fashion, her mother ignored her question. "What have I told you? If you clean up a little every day, it's not that hard to stay on top of things. A tidy house makes for a tidy mind."

Helene gave her daughter a quick hug and kiss, then walked to the kitchen. Her perfectly pressed pants topped with a tailored shirt, and matching belt and shoes made her feel dowdy in her flannel shirt and jeans. Tasha sighed as she trailed behind. Despite the fact Tasha didn't want to deal with her mother right now, she didn't have a choice.

When Tasha made it to the kitchen, she found her mother sitting at the table.

"I'd like a glass of water, please. No ice." Tasha squirmed as her mother examined her. "And get some for yourself. You're dehydrated. I can tell from the dullness of your skin. It's a tad flaky, too."

Tasha did as she was told and filled two glasses with water and brought them to the table.

"You didn't mention to me you were stopping by today. Everything okay?"

Helene looked up from her purse. Tasha saw her mother stuff a piece of paper back into the bag before she spoke.

"I was in the neighborhood and decided to drop by to see my perfect grandchildren! Where are they?"

"Perfect is going a bit far, Mom, even for you." Tasha's eyebrows raised in suspicion before she glanced at her watch. "They should be home in a few minutes."

The women spent a few minutes catching up on the week's events. Knowing she didn't have much time before the kids came home, Tasha started to question her mother's visit again but before she could get the words out the front door opened. Her children's voices filled the air.

"I told you, Blake. It was my turn."

"No, you cheated. It's my turn."

"Mom, Blake is being difficult again."

"Sounds like you and your sister at that age." Helene stood up and greeted her grandchildren with a hug.

"Hi, Grandma! Mommy, Blake got the mail, and it was my turn. The schedule says so." Libby managed to complain about her brother and hug her grandmother at the same time. "Who is that lady in the living room?"

Blake spoke before she had a chance.

"It was not her turn. She got the mail yesterday because I forgot to get it, so it really is my turn." Blake flung his backpack and an armload of mail to the ground. He broke into the embrace between his grandmother and sister. "Hi, Grandma! Move, Libby! I want to hug Grandma, too."

Tasha leaned back on the kitchen counter. She watched her mother chat with the kids, who were still arguing. The twins fought constantly. And when they weren't fighting, they talked loudly to anyone who would listen.

"Dinner at my house Saturday night, okay?" Tasha realized Helene was looking at her for an answer.

"Yeah, sure. We'll be there," said Tasha.

"We don't need you, only Libby and Blake. Drop them off at five. They can spend the night if they want."

Screams of joy erupted from the kids, and Tasha knew she had to agree.

"Sounds good. They'll be there." Tasha considered her options for a child-free Saturday night. She could have pizza delivered, watch a movie, and work on her crocheting. She sighed. Even to her, those options sounded pathetic.

"Good. You two decide what you want to eat and have your mom call me with your order." Helene hugged Blake and Libby. "We can watch a movie, too."

As Libby and Blake went to the pantry to find a snack, an argument broke out as to what movie they should watch. Tasha waited for the kids' voices to quiet down before she turned to her mother.

"So that's why you came over? To invite the kids for a sleepover?"

"You deserve a night off. I'm being a good mother and grandmother."

Tasha frowned. "You're sure there's nothing else going on?"

"Stop being so suspicious and say thank you like a good daughter." Helene called goodbye to her grandchildren and headed out the door. "See you Saturday."

Tasha knew following her mother would do no good, so she bent down to pick up the mail Blake had dropped. She tossed the junk mail and grocery circular in the recycle can and put the bill on the counter with the mail she'd sorted earlier. Just looking at the pile reminded her of the letter from Doug.

Pulling it from the bottom of the pile, she reread it. Her hands trembled as her anger built.

"How could Doug do this?" she said to the empty kitchen. "What an ass—" Tasha cut herself off before she finished the sentence, but it wasn't soon enough.

"Mommy, what did you say?" Libby poked her head out of the pantry.

"She said 'ass' and now I get to, too." Blake appeared with a granola bar in his hand. "What an ass, what an ass, what an ass!" Blake sang the sentence as he began tearing open the wrapper.

"Okay, just because I say something doesn't mean you get to say it, too." From experience, she knew Blake would repeat the word for the rest of the afternoon. It irritated her she'd forgotten they were in the pantry, but the cease and desist order had distracted her. The tactic was a low blow, even for Doug.

Libby interrupted her thoughts.

"Mommy, I'm going to my room. I have homework to do. And I have a new book I want to read." With that, Libby marched out of the kitchen.

Tasha looked at Blake. "What about you? Any homework?"

"Spelling. Why do I have to spell?" Blake's shoulders slumped. "I can use spellcheck on the computer. I hate spelling."

"Tell you what. Go do your spelling, and after I finish with the mail, I'll come play Legos with you."

Blake smiled, then looked toward the stack of mail. "Did Daddy send me the new Lego set he promised?"

Tasha forced a smile, pushing down the anger she felt toward her ex-husband. Doug disappointed his son. He made promises he didn't keep, but nothing she did changed his behavior. She hated watching how sad Blake was but felt powerless to do anything about it.

"No, buddy. No new Legos."

Blake nodded. "He must be busy. He said he would send them. Okay, come play with me when you're done." He shuffled out of the kitchen, dragging his backpack behind him.

Seeing Blake disappointed broke her heart. Libby didn't seem to mind her father's absence, but Tasha still worried about the long-term impact of the divorce. One thing was for sure: it was time to talk to Doug again about stepping up to his duties. He may not need his kids, but they needed him.

A problem for another day, thought Tasha. The current problem was right in front of her.

Sitting down at the table, Tasha began to read. She made it to the second page before she realized Doug's name wasn't on the document.

Her former fertility specialist's was.

3

T asha could not believe what she was reading. Dr.
Purdue, the IVF specialist whose handiwork created
her son and daughter, accused her of spreading lies.
She hadn't even thought of the man for years. Why would a
successful doctor come at her? Sure, Doug created a ruckus
after the kids were born. The housecleaner's assessment of the
situation was accurate. But that situation was entirely Doug's
doing, not hers. She never participated in any of the news
conferences where Doug accused Dr. Purdue of mixing up their
embryos with another couple's.

Taking a deep breath and closing her eyes, Tasha counted
to ten. She knew there had to be a reasonable explanation for
this, although anything to do with Doug was complicated. She
opened her eyes, feeling somewhat calmer. Determined to
figure out the reason for the letter, she slowly and methodically
reread it.

The letter stated Dr. Purdue's office routinely reviewed
several medical ratings websites. During an assessment, several
one-star reviews claimed Dr. Purdue knowingly switched

patients' embryos. The doctor denied the switch and refused to do anything about it despite being presented with DNA proof.

Tasha continued reading.

Dr. Purdue stands against unfounded and untrue patient complaints. He is aggressively defending his professional status from these unsubstantiated accusations.

Ms. Gerome, this is your only notification to cease complaining about Dr. Purdue's practice. If you choose not to cease your activity, we will be forced to file a defamation lawsuit against you.

Thank you and have a nice day.

"Have a nice day? How twisted can you get?"

Tasha rested her head in her hands as she thought about how this could have happened. Unable to come up with any explanation for the accusations, Tasha tossed the paperwork on the table and reached for her phone. She dialed the number of Smith, Rogers, Shaw LLC by memory and picked up her water glass. Tasha waited for an answer as she filled the glass with water.

"Good afternoon, Smith, Rogers, Shaw. Hi, Tasha," Renee, the receptionist, answered. "How's it going? Wait. Don't answer that. You're calling for an attorney. I already know the answer. Bill's in a meeting right now. Can I take a message?"

Renee's rapid-fire speech unsettled some clients, but Tasha didn't mind it.

"Nope, this is important. Is Rich around?"

"No, he's busy, too."

Tasha paused. Normally, she wouldn't consider talking with Shaw. She and Shaw had a long, colorful history, but Tasha knew she needed to address this complaint sooner rather than later. With resignation in her voice, Tasha asked, "Is Sara available?"

Renee went silent. If she wasn't so stressed-out, Tasha would have joked this was the first time she knew Renee to be lost for words. Instead, she waited for Renee to recover.

"Sure. Can you hold a minute? Let me see if she's available."

"Yes, I can hold." Tasha picked at the cuticle on her thumb as she listened to the hold music. It sounded like the same music from eight years ago. Right after she won the lottery Tasha spent hours on hold, waiting for answers on how to claim the lottery winnings with the minimal amount of disruption to her and Doug's lives.

Some of the strategies worked. The attorneys set up trust accounts and introduced her to reliable financial planners. Her money was protected, and Tasha never needed to work again. Other strategies backfired. No one foresaw Doug's public meltdown and extramarital affair. A post nuptial agreement might have helped, but in the end, Doug left with half of the money and a vague promise about visiting his kids.

Tasha knew Sara helped with the case, but they'd never talked about it. The experience was embarrassing enough for Tasha. Sara never outgrew her love of making Tasha squirm when she got into situations like this. Needless to say, Tasha preferred to work with Bill and Rich.

The hold music stopped when Sara picked up her extension.

"Hello, Tasha. How is my little sister today?"

"Great. Just great." Tasha watched the blood drip from her thumb as she tore off the last of the cuticle.

"That's debatable, isn't it? You're calling your attorney's office, so things can't really be great, now can they?"

"Oh, I thought we were sharing pleasantries." Tasha sucked the blood from her thumb. "I didn't realize you're ready to get down to business."

"What is that noise? Never mind. I'm billing you by the quarter hour. What's the issue?"

Tasha took a deep breath to prepare herself. And, with as much detail as possible, she explained the situation to her sister. Sara interrupted a few times to ask questions, but it didn't take long for Sara to get up to speed.

"So, what do we do?" Tasha finished up. "Any suggestions?"

"Did you write those reviews?"

"No," Tasha said. "I wasn't even the one who complained about him in the first place. Doug was."

"Do you think Doug did it?"

Tasha grabbed a paper towel to wrap around her still-bleeding thumb before she answered.

"Maybe. But I don't know why he'd go out of his way to give the guy a bad review. I mean, Doug said his piece on national television years ago. At this point, there's nothing in it for Doug, so why would he bother?"

"When was the last time you talked to Doug?"

Tasha pressed her index finger into her temple and made tiny circles. She felt a tension headache coming on, which would not help the situation.

"About a month ago. China's latest gifts for the twins irritated me, and I snapped."

"What did the husband-stealing bimbo send this time? I won't bill you for this part. I'm just curious."

"A sequined halter top and matching short-shorts to Libby." Tasha cringed at the memory of the outfit. "Apparently, she wants Libby to follow in her footsteps and be a stripper."

"What did she send Blake? Wait. Don't tell me. Let me guess." Sara snorted. "A blow-up doll?"

Tasha smiled for the first time since she opened the letter.

"Nothing quite that bad. Just a motorcycle."

"What's wrong with a toy motorcycle?"

"No. A custom-built motorcycle Blake's size. The gift card said he should be careful when riding it to school." Tasha remembered how disappointed Blake was when she told him he couldn't keep it. "She didn't realize Blake needs a driver's license to ride it, but whatever."

"Wow. While that explains the snapping, we—and by we, I mean you—have a problem." Sara returned to lawyer mode. "So, if you didn't write anything, and assuming Doug didn't either, why would the doctor have blamed you? You're positive you haven't talked to anyone recently about Dr. Purdue?"

Tasha sat up straight when a thought popped into her head.

"Hey, I did have a conversation with a nurse at the pediatrician's office, but I can't believe how it would play into any of this."

Sara sighed.

"Tasha, we've been through this before. Anything and everything can cause legal trouble." Even without being in front of her sister, Tasha knew Sara's pen was poised over a legal notepad. "What exactly was said and by whom?"

Clearing her throat, Tasha thought about the last visit to the pediatrician. A nurse she'd never met before took them back to the exam room. Tasha remembered some of the questions the nurse asked seemed weird.

"The office switched to a new, paperless system. The intake nurse asked me a bunch of questions about the kids' history. When I mentioned we saw Dr. Purdue, she got all excited. I guess she used to work for the guy and figured I was a fan as well."

"What did you say to her?"

Struggling to remember exactly how she responded, Tasha shrugged.

"What was I supposed to say in front of the kids? That the pompous ass of a doctor verbally promised Doug two boys even though his paperwork made no guarantees? How is that supposed to make Libby feel?"

"Point taken. It was an uncomfortable position to be in," said Sara. "But I need you to think about the conversation. Could this woman have gotten the wrong impression?"

Tasha's mind went blank.

"I really don't know. I don't remember saying anything other than we appreciated his help. I was more concerned with keeping Blake from bouncing off the ceiling. The doctor's office isn't his favorite place." Something dawned on Tasha. "Wait a minute. The nurse acted weird when she realized Doug was my ex."

"Did she say anything specific?"

Tasha frowned as she recalled the scene in the doctor's office.

The nurse looked up from the file and said, "You're the one married to that lunatic who went on national television and maligned poor Dr. Purdue."

Blake interrupted.

"What is malign, Mommy?"

Before Tasha could explain, Libby piped up, "To malign someone is to say something bad about that person. Daddy said something bad about that doctor, didn't he, Mommy?"

Holding up a hand, Tasha said, "Blake. Libby. Hold on. Daddy said what he thought was right at the time. He apologized." Turning to the nurse, Tasha continued. "I'm no longer married to Doug. He and I split up several years ago."

Sara interrupted Tasha's stroll down memory lane.

"That could be it. If that woman has some sort of connection to Dr. Purdue, she might have gone back to him, saying you're still holding a grudge. There are a number of cases right now where doctors are fighting back against patients who complain about them. You might be in the middle of something like that. Bring me the letter, and I'll draft a response. I don't think this will go further, but we need to respond quickly. Are the paternity test results in the kids' medical records?"

"Yes." Tasha closed her eyes at the memory of Doug's temper tantrums after the children were conceived. Despite the doctor's best intentions to implant two male embryos, IVF produced a boy and a girl. For months, Doug threatened, pouted, yelled, and whined after he found out he wasn't getting two boys. "Do you remember how Doug wouldn't stop referring to them as my son Blake and his sister Libby?"

"How could I forget? The man would not shut up about it."

Clicking from Sara's keyboard reached Tasha's ears. "I never understood why he was so upset, though. No infant looks like its parents. It resembles a shriveled prune after labor and delivery."

"Thank you. It makes me feel better knowing my children looked like dried fruit."

"They don't look like fruit now. And, if Doug hadn't made a big deal about Libby, you wouldn't have the DNA evidence showing that Dr. Purdue did not mix up your children, so you have no motivation to post bad reviews about him."

Tasha considered what her sister said. "Then I guess it's a good thing Doug's an idiot or we wouldn't have DNA proof."

"Good point. Okay, bring me the letter. I'll email you if I need anything else." Sara paused. "Hey, Tasha?"

"What?"

"Don't tell anyone about this. Anyone. No need to give Dr. Purdue any ammunition. Do you understand?"

"Got it. I won't say a word." Tasha forced the next sentence out of her mouth before she could change her mind. "Sara, thank you for helping me."

"Don't worry about it. My bill is in the mail." The line disconnected.

Tasha replaced the phone in its cradle. She gently pulled the paper towel from her thumb and examined the damage. Dried blood stained the towel, and her cuticle was in shreds. Tasha hoped this mess got resolved fast. Otherwise, she was going to need a lot of manicures.

4

T asha pushed the stack of clean clothes off her bed as she pulled down her comforter.

"Why didn't I have the housecleaner fold those?" Tasha asked herself. "Oh, that's right. I told her I could do it myself."

Sighing at her lack of motivation, she walked into the bathroom to brush her teeth. She was exhausted from getting the kids' medical files ready for Sara. That wasn't entirely true, she thought, as she squeezed out the toothpaste. Worrying about the letter from the IVF doctor drained her.

The electric toothbrush vibrated in her mouth as she kicked off her shoes. The tennis shoes landed in the corner, next to several other pairs of shoes waiting to return to the closet. She sat on the edge of the bathtub, pushing aside several damp bath towels while the toothbrush did its job and thought about that last trip to the pediatrician.

Did she forget to tell Sara something? She went through the entire visit in her mind again. It had been unpleasant from the start.

"BLAKE, please get out from behind there." Tasha pushed her hair out of her eyes as she asked her son for the third time. Her argument with China that morning exhausted her. That and the fact a visit to the pediatrician's office was never fun tried Tasha's patience. "The doctor will be in here any second, and you need to be on the table. Don't make me pull you out from behind there."

Her son's head popped out from behind the table.

"I don't like sitting on that paper thingy. It's crinkly. And there's hidden treasure back here." He pushed several tongue depressors out from where he was hiding. "I'm a pirate. Argh."

Trying not to think about how many germs grew on the wooden sticks, Tasha bent down and took Blake's hand. She squeezed it and gently pulled.

"I know this isn't any fun, buddy, but you have to get your check-up," she said as her son's body appeared. She brushed off the dust covering the knees of Blake's jeans. Shaking her head, she made a mental note to ask the front desk to give the room a thorough cleaning. "Plus, Libby's getting hers, too."

Tasha glanced over her shoulder at her daughter who was sitting quietly reading her book. At the sound of her name, Libby looked up and smiled.

"Who's more fun to take to the doctor, Mommy? Me or Blake?"

Resisting the desire to roll her eyes, Tasha said, "You know the answer, Libby. You're both fun to bring. Just different." She squirted hand sanitizer on her hands and rubbed them together. She turned to put some on Blake's hands, but he wasn't standing next to her. He'd moved back to the exam table and managed to pull out the stirrups that were built into the end.

Sending up a silent prayer Blake or Libby didn't ask about

the leg supports, she approached the table and showed Blake how to put them away. This time, she held Blake's hand as she led him to the bench and squirted a large dollop of sanitizer in his palm.

"Okay, rub your hands together. Those treasures of yours were kinda dirty."

As Blake attempted to rub his hands together, there was a knock at the door.

"About time," Tasha uttered under her breath before saying, "Come in."

Tasha expected to see Dr. Henderson enter, but a woman she didn't recognize came into the exam room instead.

"Hello. I'm Nurse Judi. I'm here to take vital signs." Before Tasha could react, Blake dove behind the exam table. The nurse pointed at Libby. "Let's start with you."

Placing her bookmark in its place, Libby closed her book, and crawled up on the exam table.

"I'll get Blake," Tasha said as she got back down on her hands and knees and poked her head around the side of the table. "Hey, Blake. I need you out here, buddy. The sooner you get out here, the sooner we can go home."

"But I don't like her," Blake said, and Tasha cringed. It was never a good idea to publicly announce you don't like the nurse who would be administering shots. *He'll have to learn the hard way*, she thought. "I want the other lady. The one with the pigs."

Tasha liked the nurse who wore the scrubs covered with flying pigs, too, but all she wanted to do now was finish up this appointment. Grabbing his size one sneaker, Tasha pulled her son toward her.

"She's not here, Blake. Nurse Judi is helping us today." Tasha picked her son up and sat down in the chair Libby vacated. Blake squirmed in her lap, but Tasha held him tight. She had no desire to fish him out from behind the table again.

Nurse Judi wrapped the blood pressure cuff around Libby's arm. "Just going to give your arm a little squeeze. Sit as still as you can."

Libby did as she was told while Blake struggled in his mother's arms.

"I don't like that thing. It hurts my arm. Is she going to hurt my arm?"

Using one arm to subdue Blake, Tasha reached into her purse with her free hand to find something to distract him. She gave a sigh of relief when her hand came into contact with a race car tucked away in the bottom. Pulling out the car, she showed it to Blake.

"Hey, why don't you play with this while you wait your turn?"

Blake took the car in his hands and plopped down on the floor. He pushed the toy around the room, making car noises as he gathered more dirt on his knees.

The nurse nodded down at Blake.

"A couple of years makes all the difference, doesn't it? Plus, girls always mature faster."

Tasha's eyebrows came together into the middle of her forehead.

"What do you mean? Blake and Libby are twins. They're the same age."

The look on Nurse Judi's face was priceless. Her eyes widened to the size of Libby's American Girl doll's eyes. Then, her mouth puckered into a perfect "o" shape. It reminded Tasha of a meme she saw a few days ago of a Swedish yodeler who lost her voice.

The woman looked from Libby to Blake. Libby sat patiently on the table, while Blake yelled "Stop that car! It's getting away!" as he pushed the hot rod behind the exam table.

"Are you sure? They don't look anything alike."

Tasha struggled to control her temper. It was bad enough

non-medical people gave her a hard time about fraternal twins. But this was a medical professional. This woman had to know how fraternal twins happened, didn't she?

"And their personalities are completely opposite," said the nurse. "There's no way they're twins."

Tasha's self-control began to slip. She hated explaining Libby and Blake were twins. She also hated bringing the kids to the doctor. Tasha sat back in the chair and crossed her arms over her chest.

"You know, if you look in the file, you'll see the information on Dr. Purdue. It's all in there." Pleased with her response, Tasha looked around to see if Libby or Blake were paying attention. Neither of the kids seemed to notice the conversation. When Tasha turned back to the nurse, she was surprised to see the nurse's cheeks flushed.

"Dr. Purdue? Really? He is the best reproductive endocrinologist in the tri-state area. I worked for him briefly. How did you get in to see him? He's booked out for years."

Tasha debated how to answer the question. The truth was Doug used the publicity from their lottery win to strong-arm their way into the office. She didn't want to tell Nurse Judi that. Instead, she settled for a neutral answer.

"We got lucky, I guess." Tasha shrugged and hoped the look on her face conveyed sincerity.

"You hit the jackpot is what you did," Nurse Judi said, unaware of the double meaning of her statement. "Dr. Purdue is fabulous. A miracle worker. He gets more women pregnant than—well, he gets a lot of women pregnant. Wasn't he great to work with?"

Judi waited like a child on Christmas morning for Tasha's response.

Great. If you like a doctor with a God-complex. He basically ruined my marriage. Wait, that's not right. He sped up the ruin of my marriage.

"Yeah, I appreciate everything he did for me. Without him, I wouldn't have Blake and Libby." Hoping to change the subject, Tasha asked, "So do the kids need shots this appointment?"

Nurse Judi looked back down at the chart and frowned. She stared for longer than was necessary before focusing back on Tasha.

"Gerome? Hey, that's the name of the guy who won the lottery." When Tasha didn't respond, Nurse Judi continued. "Are you married to that lunatic who went on national television and maligned poor Dr. Purdue?"

TASHA spat the toothpaste into the sink and rinsed her mouth. Watching her reflection in the mirror, she remembered the rest of the appointment. Nurse Judi was short with the children and rude to her. The tension in the room was uncomfortable. Tasha was relieved when Nurse Judi left, slamming the door behind her.

Tears pricked at her eyes when she remembered what Blake said.

"She's not as nice as the nurse with pigs. Can we have her next time?"

Tasha nodded at her son.

"I hope so, buddy. I certainly hope so."

5

Pulling into the parking lot of Smith, Rogers, Shaw LLC the next morning, Tasha let out a deep sigh. She didn't get much sleep the night before. Tasha tossed and turned, worrying about the Dr. Purdue situation. The dull ache in her head begged for pain relief, but she'd forgotten to snag some ibuprofen on her way out of the house.

It didn't help matters that she was at the scene of her nasty divorce negotiations. When people said that divorce sucked, it was an understatement. Tasha thought of it like nine levels of hell.

A group of moms pushing strollers caught her attention. She knew they were heading to the park a few blocks away and she wished she could join them. The park reminded her of happier times with her family. Doug's brother, Brad, designed the park and picnic structures a few years earlier. It was one of the few times Doug supported his brother. They all should have known better. But Doug's presentation to the city council planning board sucked them all in.

"Brad's design is an important addition to the community. This is a place I want my kids to enjoy. Not only is it safe, the picnic building, and surrounding structures add a little flair to things. It's definitely better than what any of the neighboring communities have."

After Brad's firm won the bid on the park, a huge argument arose between the brothers. She tipped her head back against the headrest as she remembered the fight. Doug demanded his brother put him in charge of the project for his part in securing the bid.

"I can't put you in charge of the construction crew, Doug. You don't have the skills or experience," Brad explained. "If you want to work another job, that's fine. But this government contract is my chance to prove I can handle the work. You're not ready for that."

That argument was the turning point in the brothers' relationship. Doug never forgave Brad for not giving him the job and their relationship was never the same. It got so bad that Doug stopped going to family events where Brad might be. Tasha still missed Brad's sense of humor at family dinners.

Shaking her head to clear it, Tasha wondered what Brad would say about her current situation.

"You know, getting a cease and desist letter from a high-profile doctor doesn't happen to every girl." She imagined him winking at her as he continued. "Doug would be thrilled with all the attention."

Her mother hadn't found the positive of the situation. Helene questioned her reasoning during their evening phone call the night before.

"I don't care who it is, young lady. You are in trouble," said Helene. "What in the world were you thinking, writing a bad review about a doctor? Doctors deserve respect."

Tasha wondered again why she told her mother. Helene believed anyone with an advanced degree, like a MD or JD, walked on water. That could be why Helene considered Sara the more successful of her daughters.

Rather than ruminate about something she couldn't change, Tasha hopped out of the minivan. The receptionist's desk overlooked the parking lot. Renee would wonder why she was sitting in her minivan. As Tasha took a step toward the building, she heard an oinking sound.

"You're kidding me." She looked down. She had forgotten to put on shoes. Instead, she wore the fluffy pink pig slippers the kids had given her for Mother's Day. The slippers oinked with every step she made. Tasha loved them, even loved the oinking. She didn't want everyone in Sara's office to know about her oinking pig slippers, though. *Too late now*, she thought and continued to the door.

The door's chime announced her arrival, and Renee smiled broadly.

"Good morning, Tasha. How are you today?"

What a dumb question. I'm standing in a law firm wearing pig slippers, dropping off a cease and desist order. How do you think my day is going?

Tasha sighed and plastered what she hoped was a pleasant expression on her face.

"Great, how are you? How's roller derby going?" Tasha hoped if she distracted Renee, she wouldn't have to explain the pig slippers. She was also curious. Tasha didn't watch roller derby, but she wouldn't mind ramming someone right now.

"Great, thanks for asking. We're in second place right now because we beat the Girls of Combat. Tough jams last night. I have the bandages to prove it." Renee lifted her arms. She wore several hot-pink bandages covered in cartoon cats.

"Wow. Libby would love those. I'll have to get some. I'm down to boy bandages at our house." Tasha wiggled her hand for Renee to see. A bandage covered in red race cars protected her chewed-up thumb. "Is Sara in? I brought the paperwork she wanted."

"You sure know how to cause a ruckus. Dr. Purdue is only the preeminent reproductive endocrinologist in the country."

"So I hear," Tasha mumbled.

"What? Oh never mind." Renee reached for the phone. "Sara's in. I'll let her know you're here."

"I'm right here, Renee." Sara appeared in the foyer. "Tasha, come on back."

Tasha said goodbye to Renee and followed her sister down the hall. Her pig slippers oinked, but Sara didn't say anything. When they got to the door, Tasha saw Sara's office was pristine, as usual. Neat stacks of files sat on the credenza next to the sand Zen garden Libby and Blake gave their aunt for her birthday.

"I thought we weren't supposed to discuss the situation with anyone." Tasha made a mental note to tell Libby and Blake their aunt kept their gift in her office. "Why did you tell Renee?"

"I wondered the same thing when Renee mentioned it to me. Apparently, you called Mom last night, and Mom shared your news with everyone at Betty's this morning."

Tasha groaned at the mention of Betty's Coffee Bar, the town's gossip headquarters. She avoided the place, but Helene stopped in daily to get the latest scoop and a shot of caffeine. Tasha should have known better than to tell her mother about the letter, especially after Sara's warning.

"So, who knows? With my luck, I bet the entire town knows."

"You're lucky. Slow morning. Renee and Betty were the only two there. I already talked to Betty. She agreed to take your gossip to the grave. For a price."

"What does she want? Please tell me I don't have to play catcher for her?" For years, Betty begged Tasha to play for the Coffee Bar's softball team. Tasha always refused for fear of being run over at home plate. "Anything but that."

"You agreed to buy the team new uniforms and equipment for next season. I thought it was fair." Sara pointed a finger at her sister. "Keep your mouth shut. If Purdue's attorneys are any good, they will be looking for proof this was you. I can only do so much damage control. Understand?"

"Yes, I got it. Here's the letter." Tasha wished she had never opened her mouth—to anyone. "I also grabbed my file on the kids. The paternity tests are there. Plus their birth certificates, our marriage license, divorce certificate, and custody agreement."

"I shouldn't need all that stuff," said Sara, "but I'm glad you have it easily accessible."

Tasha didn't bother to tell her sister how long it took her to find all the papers. She knew that would cause a lecture on the importance of organization. Tasha didn't have the patience to listen to that now.

Sara took the file and set it on her desk. "I'll let you know if I need anything else, but for now, please don't say anything else about this. I cannot stress enough how important it is to be quiet. And you need to call Mom and tell her not to tell anyone else."

Tasha turned to leave. "Why didn't you call her? You talked to Betty."

"I went to Betty's for coffee, so it was convenient. And if I call Mom, she's going to ask me if I'm dating. And I don't have time, nor do I want to deal with that right now. Your mess. Your call."

Tasha followed Sara back to the reception area. On the phone, Renee waved goodbye to Tasha. Tasha made it to the door, relieved no one commented on her oinking footwear when her sister called her name. Tasha looked back over her shoulder.

"Those are some awesome pig slippers." Sara smiled and winked. "Where can I get a pair?"

Tasha shook her head and stuck her tongue out at her sister. She deserved the comment, but she wasn't going to stick around for any more of Sara's teasing. As Tasha spun back to the door, her pig slippers lost traction. Her feet flew out from under her, and Tasha grabbed at anything to stop her fall. She managed to snag the coat tree, but instead of stopping her fall, the wooden rack came down with her. As she hit the floor, she heard both Renee and Sara calling her name.

Dazed and breathless, Tasha lay on the hardwood floor. She stayed still, processing what had happened, and scanning her body for injuries. Nothing hurt until she tried to sit up. A shooting pain careened down her neck to her shoulder and into her arm, so she lay back and closed her eyes.

"Tasha, look at me. Tasha, are you okay?" Sara asked her. "Can you get up?"

"I don't think you should move her. She could have a head injury," said Renee. "One of the jammers on my team hit her head, skated the rest of the half, and then ended up in the hospital with a concussion. Let's call an ambulance."

Tasha started to say she didn't want an ambulance when she heard a third voice. The smooth, velvety tone that would be perfect for radio work or voice-overs had her eyes open in a second.

"I don't know what a jammer is, but she didn't hit that hard," Brad said, smiling down at her. "How about some help up?"

6

Brad squatted next to Tasha. He arrived in the lobby as Tasha's slipper-covered feet slid out from under her. Even though she didn't hit her head, Brad checked her pupils like his high school football coach taught him. Her eyes were normal, but he noticed Tasha grabbed her right arm when she struggled to sit up.

Sara's voice interrupted his assessment.

"Renee, call 911." She sounded shaky. "She's in so much pain, she's moaning. That can't be good."

Brad saw the look of pain that crossed Tasha's face when she lifted her right hand.

"It's okay. I'm dying of embarrassment," said Tasha. "Don't call an ambulance. Someone help me up."

Avoiding the right side of her body, Brad helped Tasha to her feet. He stood next to her for a few seconds to make sure she was steady. Tasha wobbled at first but regained her balance. When Brad let go, his hand accidentally knocked into her right arm. She turned her head, but not before Brad glimpsed the tortured look on her face.

She's in pain, but she isn't going to admit it.

"There's nothing to be embarrassed about," said Brad. He looked up at Renee and Sara. "Could she get some water and ibuprofen? She's going to need it."

His request startled the two other women into action.

"I've got the water," said Renee, rushing down the hall.

"I've got both ibuprofen and naproxen in my office." Sara frowned at her sister. "Doesn't ibuprofen bother your stomach?"

Brad answered for Tasha.

"Bring them both. Tasha can decide in a minute. The sooner she takes them, the sooner they'll kick in."

Nodding, Sara followed Renee out of the lobby. As soon as the women were gone, Brad felt Tasha's body relax.

"Thanks for sending them on an errand. I don't need an audience."

He grinned.

"Same old Tasha I see. Never wanting to admit she needs help. Let's get you to the couch." As he put one hand on her back, Brad felt Tasha's body stiffen. Guiding her to the couch, Brad released her hand as she sat down. "It's not your head that hurts, is it?"

"My head's fine. It's this stupid shooting pain in my shoulder," she replied. She glanced up at him with a groan. "I shouldn't have told you that. You'll tell Sara, and I'll spend the day at the doctor's office."

Brad shook his head. "Follow my lead. I'll take care of you."

The women rushed back into the lobby. Renee carried a bottle of water while Sara gripped several small bottles of pain medication.

"How is she? I brought all the pain meds from my office and the ones in the kitchen." Sara held them out to Brad. "What do you think would work best?"

Remind me never to get hurt around this woman. She's a basket case, and there isn't even any blood. God help her if she ever has kids.

Confident Tasha was shaken up and not seriously injured, Brad took the ibuprofen bottle from Sara and shook out two tablets. He handed them to Tasha, and Renee gave her the water. No one said anything for a minute while Tasha downed the pain relievers, but Brad could see Sara fidgeting.

Time to get Tasha out of here before Sara drives her to the ER.

"You guys don't have to stand over me. I'm fine. I can handle it. It's my own fault." Tasha looked down at the pink pigs on her feet. "I should've worn shoes. I'll be sore tomorrow."

"As if that's the worst of your problems," Sara said. Brad wondered what she meant, but before he could ask, Sara continued, "Do you think you can drive?"

Brad jumped on the opportunity. She would never see a doctor on her own, but if he took her directly to Carlton's office, Tasha wouldn't have a choice.

"I can drive her home. She's got a pretty hard head, but someone should watch her for a while. To be sure," Brad said. He smiled when he added, "If that's okay with you, Tasha. You could always call your mother."

The look of disapproval on Sara's face made him frown.

"Do you think that's a good idea, Brad? Doug was adamant Tasha can't be around his family anymore. He'd throw a fit if he saw this." Sara waved her arms around the room to indicate their current situation. "The last time he found out the kids visited his mother, Doug's attorney sent Tasha a nasty letter."

Tucking his hands into his jeans pockets, Brad said, "My stupid brother can't tell me who I can or can't see. He divorced her. Which was the dumbest freakin' thing he's ever done and that's saying a lot. Besides, neither of you have time to spare today, do you?"

From the sheepish looks he received he knew he was in the clear.

"Are you sure you have time?" said Tasha. "You must have a meeting or something going on."

"Finished. I wrapped things up here, so I am available to help my favorite sister-in-law in her time of need."

"I had no idea I was your favorite ex-sister-in-law," Tasha corrected. "But as long as you're sure it's not an inconvenience, I'll take you up on the offer."

7

Brad walked her down the office steps. The oinking of her slippers accompanied them on their walk to his truck. Despite the absurdity of the situation, Tasha was happy to see him.

"Here we are." Brad opened the passenger door and stepped out of the way. Tasha managed to climb into the cab on her own, with minimal pain in her shoulder. She relaxed back onto the soft, worn leather seat as Brad closed the door.

Leave it to me to turn a simple trip to the attorney's office into a disaster.

If she could just hang on a little while longer, she would be home soon to wallow in self-pity and embarrassment.

The driver's door creaked open. Brad slid into the seat and started the mammoth pickup truck which shook as the engine came to life, jarring the front seat. Pain shot down into her hand. She bit the inside of her lip to keep from gasping out loud.

"Are you going to be honest with me about how much pain you're in? If not, I'm taking you straight to the emergency room." Brad dug his cell phone out of his pocket.

"Hey, you told me to follow your lead, and you'd take care of things," Tasha said. She didn't want to admit she needed her arm looked at. "That means you're taking me home, right?"

"You're hurt. You flinched when I helped you off the ground. You crawled into the truck like an old woman." He stared at Tasha. "Starting the truck made you gasp in pain. And your face is ghost white. Don't tell me you're fine."

"Damn it, I thought I did a better job of acting," said Tasha in frustration. "Take me home. I'm embarrassed enough. I don't need to go to the hospital. I'll be fine."

Brad sat back in his seat. He didn't say anything at first, but then he shook his head.

"Look, I don't want to tell you what to do, but you need to have your shoulder looked at. You don't have to go to the hospital; I'll take you to my chiropractor." Brad held up his phone. "I'll text him. He might be able to squeeze you in. Don't you remember what happened the time you cut your hand making French fries? You almost lost your finger as you waited so long to see the doctor."

Tasha rolled her eyes at the reminder of the smelly pus that had dripped out of her swollen finger.

"Fine. Have it your way."

Brad smiled, then tapped out a message on his phone. Hoping the chiropractor was busy, Tasha sulked while they waited for a response. They didn't wait long when Brad's phone beeped, signaling a reply. He chuckled at the text before saying, "You're in luck. He can see you right now."

He put the phone in the cup holder and backed out of the parking spot.

"So, problems with Doug?" Brad put the truck in drive. "He sent you a letter, I take it. Interesting you're working with Sara."

She couldn't tell Brad the truth. Sara was adamant that she tell no one else. Tasha felt bad, though. She didn't want Brad to get the impression his brother was up to something. The brothers might talk, and the last thing she needed was for Doug to know that Brad was giving her a ride home.

"No problem. Some loose ends to clear up." Tasha hoped she sounded more confident than she felt. "Bill and Rich were busy, so Sara's helping me out. How have you been?"

She looked out the window as they drove and enjoyed the scenery. Tasha liked the perspective from Brad's truck. Her seat was higher than the seat in her minivan, so everything looked different.

"I started some work for the hospital. They're adding a reflection pond and ramada. Should be an interesting project. Great space." Brad flipped on his turn signal. "How are the kids?"

"Good. Libby loves school, and Blake is still into Legos." The twins missed their uncle. They didn't understand why they couldn't see their family. Tasha couldn't explain it either. She did remember how vile the letter was from when they visited Doug's mother, though. "They've been lobbying for a dog. I'm not sure I'm ready for that, though. Pets are a lot of work."

"Pets teach responsibility, not that Libby isn't already responsible. Blake could be in charge of walking and playing with the dog. He could burn off some of that excess energy I remember him having. A dog could keep you company during the day, too. Have you considered going to a shelter?"

"Sounds like you should get a dog."

Brad shrugged. "Sorry. I didn't mean to push."

Guilt flooded Tasha as she realized she sounded bitchy. Brad was helping her, and she gave him attitude in return.

"No, I'm sorry. I'm cranky. Now isn't a good time for a dog." Tasha straightened up as she glanced out the window. The change in position caused her arm to ache more. Swallowing a groan of pain, she asked, "Hey, why are we heading toward the hospital? I agreed to the chiropractor. I'm not going to the ER."

"Yeah, you made that clear. Don't get all worked up. My

chiropractor's office is right next to the hospital." Brad pulled into the parking lot and found a space. He parked the truck and killed the engine before turning to her. "Are you sure you're okay? I mean, I know you're in pain, but something else is bothering you. I know we aren't officially related anymore, but this picking sides stuff is crap. Whatever Doug says, I'm still your friend. You can tell me whatever's on your mind."

Silence filled the cab as Tasha stared out at the chiropractor's office. Uncomfortable, she picked at the bandage on her thumb. She debated telling Brad about the letter she'd received. She trusted Brad. He wouldn't tell anyone about what happened. At the same time, she promised Sara she wouldn't tell anyone else about Dr. Purdue.

"Earth to Tasha."

Brad's voice startled her back to reality.

"Sorry," she said, shaking her head. "As much as I'd appreciate your help, I need to figure this out on my own."

He nodded.

"I figured as much, but the offer is there if you need anything. You should head inside and have Carlton take a look at your shoulder."

"Who's Carlton?" said Tasha.

"He's the chiropractor who's staring at us right now." Brad waved to a man standing in the window. The man waved back.

Tasha automatically waved, stopping as the pain radiated down her arm.

"Wow. That hurts. I guess it's a good thing you were at Sara's today." She took off her seat belt and reached for the door handle. "Okay, I'll go. I can get home from here though. I don't want you to wait for me. You've done enough. Thanks for driving me. I appreciate it."

"Tasha, you left your minivan at Sara's office."

Tasha did a mental forehead slap.

"Oh yeah."

"I've got a couple of errands to run, but I should be finished in an hour or so. I can run you home." Brad looked up from his watch. "Plus, I haven't seen Blake or Libby in months. I can hang out and say hi when they get home from school."

The thought of how happy the kids' faces would be to see their uncle made up her mind.

"That would make their day." Brad wanted to see the kids, and Tasha wouldn't keep this opportunity from them. Doug would never know, anyway. "Okay, I'm getting out now. I'll text when I'm finished."

Gently sliding out of the truck, Tasha walked toward the office. She stumbled once when a rock from the parking lot poked through the thin soles of the pig slippers. Hopefully, Carlton the chiropractor could fix her shoulder. Then, her only concern would be a cease and desist order.

8

"L et's see if you've done any damage," Carlton said as he examined the X-rays in front of him. "Tell me again how you fell."

Tasha squirmed in her seat. Her fidgeting reminded her of Blake, only she wasn't hyperactive. Her nerves were due to the man in front of her. Brad told her Carlton was a good chiropractor, but he neglected to mention Carlton was an Adonis.

A gay Adonis judging by his perfect hair, sparkling teeth, and impeccable attire.

Chastising herself for stereotyping, Tasha cleared her throat and tucked her flyaway hair behind her ear.

"Well, these are slippery," she said pointing at the pigs on her feet. "It was a mistake to wear them, but I was in a hurry and forgot to change before I left the house. The kids gave them to me for Mother's Day, so I wear them every morning. The parenting blog I follow says children get a sense of connection when you use their gifts." Tasha knew she was babbling, but she couldn't help herself. "I know oinking pig slippers aren't a normal thing to wear, but I can't help it. I'd do anything for the kids."

The doctor nodded and frowned. Tasha thought the wrinkle on his forehead made him look even sexier.

Get a grip, woman. The man is a medical professional!

"I was looking for more description on the fall itself. Did you hit anything in particular? Your head? Elbow? That sort of thing."

Answer the question, you moron.

"Sorry," said Tasha as embarrassment washed over her. "Sometimes I get carried away. I can't say I did. My whole body hit the floor. Now my neck and arm hurt."

When the chiropractor didn't say anything, Tasha rushed on.

"Is something broken? Did I tear a tendon or muscle?" The X-ray didn't mean much to her, but she didn't see anything resembling a break. "What do you see?"

Carlton looked at her with a smile. His demeanor reminded her of a television personality rather than a doctor. He'd gone out of his way to make her feel comfortable since she'd arrived. Carlton was like no doctor she'd met before.

"The X-rays look fine. Nothing is broken. It might help if you could relax."

Tasha's face warmed, and she knew her cheeks reddened.

"Sorry. Today hasn't been my day."

Nodding his head, Carlton guided Tasha to his exam table. "So I heard."

Tilting her head, Tasha winced as her neck protested.

"Moving like that isn't a good idea," Carlton said.

"Ya think?" Tasha snorted before she caught herself. "I'm sorry. I am a nice person. I don't do well with pain."

"That's okay. Lie back." Carlton supported her as she eased back onto the table. When she was flat on her back, he tucked a pillow under her knees, then reached for her slippers. "May I?"

Realizing she was still wearing the offending slippers, Tasha nodded her head. Another flash of pain went down her arm. Despite her best efforts, a tear rolled down her cheek.

"Hey, no tears. I'll have you fixed up any minute," said Carlton. He turned and came back with a tissue. "Here."

"Thank you. This is so embarrassing," said Tasha. "I should know. I tend to do a lot of embarrassing things."

Carlton removed her slippers and turned to place them under the chair she'd been sitting in. Tasha dried her eyes while his back was turned. She planted a smile on her face by the time he returned to her side.

"Those are pretty cute as far as slippers go. I've never seen any that actually oink, though," said Carlton. "Where did your kids find them?"

"Mail order. My mom is big on knick-knacks. When the kids go over to her and Dad's, sometimes they flip through the giant stacks of catalogs."

Carlton moved Tasha's head to the side while he asked, "How old are the kids? They're twins, right?"

His comment surprised her. She didn't remember telling the chiropractor she had kids, but everything was a little vague. She noticed Carlton continued stretching out her neck as he waited for her response.

"Yes, Libby and Blake are seven," said Tasha. Curious, she asked, "Do you have kids?"

He shook his head.

"Not yet. Someday. Take a deep breath for me and blow it out to the count of five."

Tasha did as she was told. Halfway through her exhale, Carlton moved her shoulder down. A loud popping sound filled the room. Tasha gasped in surprise and automatically tensed.

"What did you do?" she asked. Then she realized something. Her arm didn't hurt. She turned her head from side to side and lifted her arm. Amazed how relaxed her body was, she looked up at Carlton. She saw a grin on his face.

"Trust me now?" Carlton stepped away from the exam table and crossed his arms. "I find this the most gratifying part of my day."

Tasha pushed herself into a sitting position. She turned her head, reveling at how loose and flexible she was. Then she pulled her arms overhead and reached to the ceiling. The pull of the stretch freed the last bit of tension in her neck and back. A softer, shorter popping sound escaped from her body, and she sighed.

"I haven't felt this good in years," Tasha said. "Really, what did you do?"

"Trade secret. If I told you, it wouldn't be a secret anymore. Now." Carlton's smile turned serious. "You haven't been taking care of yourself. I should have been able to fix this in two minutes, but it took me fifteen. You need regular adjustments. Brad told me you aren't a fan of chiropractors, but you need to take better care of yourself."

Tasha slid off the table.

"What are you doing?" The concern in Carlton's voice stopped Tasha in her tracks. "I am a miracle worker, but you need to slow down. You don't need another fall today."

"I want to stretch my back and legs," she said. "Is that okay?"

Nodding, Carlton said, "Fine. But slowly. This is a marathon. Not a sprint."

Following his instructions, she bent at the waist and dangled her arms in front of her. She reached toward the floor. "Oh my God. I haven't been able to reach my knees for years."

"If you take things slowly, you'll be able to reach the floor in a few days. Don't push it." She recognized a combination of pride and worry in his voice, and Tasha stopped where she was. It usually irritated her when people told her what to do, but

Carlton seemed different. It reminded her of the way Brad treated her. Like a sister. Whatever it was, Carlton's concern made her feel good.

She started to stand back up, but she felt a hand on her back.

"Stand up slowly. If you come up too fast, you'll get dizzy and fall again. You and I have a lot of work to do to keep you safe."

Strange as it seemed, she did feel safe. Carlton was a stranger twenty minutes ago, but something about him made her feel like she'd known him much longer.

Hanging upside down, Tasha asked, "Why are you so concerned about me, anyway?"

She thought there was hesitation between her question and his answer.

"The official answer is I'm a professional, and I care about all my patients," said Carlton. Lifting his hand from her back, he continued, "Go ahead and stand up. Slowly this time."

Tasha did as she was told and sat back down on the chair.

"Unofficially?" She tilted her head, reveling in the fact she was pain-free.

Carlton shrugged.

"Brad's a good friend. He's told me about all you've been through with his brother. I feel like I know you."

His response surprised her.

"Oh. That's nice." Tasha wondered why Brad didn't tell her he was friends with his chiropractor, but that wasn't any of her business. Instead, she decided to focus on the situation at hand. "So, what do I need to do to keep feeling this good?"

They discussed some future appointments, and Carlton handed her some brochures on stretching and yoga. As she put them in her purse, Tasha glanced at her watch.

"I better get going. The kids will be home soon." She pulled her wallet out of her purse. "How much do I owe you today?"

Carlton shook his head.

"This one's on me. I'm glad I could help."

"I can't accept that. You deserve to be paid for all the time you spent with me. Plus," she lifted both palms up and shrugged, "this was a last-minute thing."

He patted her on the arm.

"It's my pleasure. Promise me you will take care of yourself. Take some time to relax. And don't forget to come back for another visit." His face flushed a bit. "If you can convince Brad to get some work done too, that would be great."

What is that supposed to mean? thought Tasha as she put her wallet away and stretched out her arms.

"At least let me give you a *thank you* hug."

Carlton enthusiastically, but cautiously wrapped his arms around Tasha. She'd stopped rating hugs back in high school, but this would have gotten a perfect 10 on the scale. Whoever dated Carlton was one lucky man.

9

Tasha took the steps slowly, careful not to fall and mess up the miracle Carlton performed on her neck. She was pain-free, at least for now. Carlton's advice resonated in her head.

Take it easy for a couple of days. Do some light activity like walking. No heavy lifting. Don't worry about anything. Let your body heal itself.

She could follow most of his recommendations, but one. The looming Dr. Purdue situation ruined any chance of the no worry advice.

Tasha stepped into the parking lot and looked around for her minivan. Then, she remembered. Brad dropped her off. Tasha shook her head, in awe over being pain-free she'd forgotten to text Brad. Tasha pulled her phone out of her purse and called up her texts. Before she could type anything, a message from Brad popped up.

Carlton said you're ready. Finishing an errand. Be there in five.

Turning back to look at the building, Tasha stared at the empty window of Carlton's office. It was nice of him to let Brad know, but it seemed a bit odd. As a woman wearing pig slippers outside in broad daylight, she knew odd. But why would Carlton tell Brad? And why would Brad share so much information with Carlton about her and the kids? Business associates shared small talk, but this seemed a bit much to her.

Carlton's parting comment about Brad wasn't particularly professional either.

Before she came up with a good answer, her phone rang. "Come on Eileen" by Dexys Midnight Runners blasted in the parking lot. Tasha smiled. A long-time family joke, Tasha grew up thinking the lyrics were "Come on Helene". Once she understood song lyrics, it became even funnier to Tasha and her sister. It irritated Helene, which is precisely why both she and Sara used it for their mother's ringtone.

Tasha sat down on the curb as she answered her phone.

"Hi, Mom. What's up?"

"Sara said you fell. Are you okay?" Helene's voice was two pitches higher than usual. Tasha knew from experience this meant her mother was worried. "Do you need me to do anything? Wait a minute. Where are you? Shouldn't you be home by now? The kids get out of school soon."

Grinning at her mom's concern, Tasha said, "I'm fine. You don't need to do anything. I'm sitting outside a chiropractor's office, and I've got plenty of time before the bus arrives." She waited for her words to sink in, and she wasn't disappointed.

"Chiropractor?! I've tried to get you to go for years. Since when did you start going to a chiropractor?" She stopped to catch her breath. "Oh my God. You had a traumatic brain injury. The nightly news says those change your personality. Don't sign any legal documents! In your state, it could be dangerous. Give me the address of where you are, and I'll come to get you."

As she started to answer, Brad's truck pulled into the parking lot. He stopped right in front of her and hopped out.

Walking to Tasha's side, he said, "Sorry, I'm late. My errand took longer than I expected. Ready to go?"

Helene let out a screech, and Tasha pulled the phone away from her ear.

"Was that Brad's voice? What in the world is going on? Sara has a lot of explaining to do."

Brad's brow crinkled at the sound of Helene's voice. He offered his hand to help Tasha off the curb. She shook her head and hopped up on her own power. She grinned at the look on his face before walking to the truck. Tasha opened the door and slid pain-free into the passenger's seat.

"Mom, Brad's here to take me home so I can't talk." Tasha sat back in the seat, relieved she didn't have to explain what happened. "I'll call you later."

"You better, Natasha Gerome. Because I'm calling Sara right now to find out what in the world is going on!"

Helene disconnected without a goodbye, and Tasha slid the phone back into her purse. Turning to look at Brad as he got into the truck, she said, "As if you didn't hear, that was my mom. She was a bit surprised to find out where I'd been today."

"So I heard. How is Helene doing these days?" asked Brad as he started the engine. "It's been a while since I've seen her."

Tasha glanced out the window of the truck and noticed Carlton's face peering out the window. Turning back to Brad, she saw him looking at Carlton as well. An idea took shape, but Tasha kept it to herself. Instead, she answered Brad's question.

"She's doing fine. Always wants to help with the kids. Right now her life's mission is to set me up with someone. She has it in her head I need a boyfriend." She let the word linger in the air, but Brad didn't respond. He put the truck in gear and headed toward the road. "Do you think I need a boyfriend?"

Brad flicked on his blinker before turning.

"I don't know. Do you want a boyfriend?"

Tasha felt like a teenager. She didn't need anyone meddling

in her love life, including her ex-brother-in-law. Even if she was curious about his.

"No. Not particularly. Right now, all I want to do is be home before the kids. I don't want to explain what happened today. Blake would think it was funny that I fell in the slippers, but Libby worries too much," she said. Changing the subject, Tasha asked, "Did you get your errand done?"

He nodded toward the backseat.

"I did. I hope you're okay with what I got."

Confused, Tasha turned around and looked behind her. Sitting on the bench seat were two boxes. One contained a Lego set, and the other boasted a STEM construction set. Tasha recognized Brad's handwriting on the cards sitting next to the boxes.

"You didn't have to do that."

Brad nodded and said, "I wanted to get them something." She noticed he kept his eyes on the road when he asked, "I'd like to stick around this afternoon if you don't mind. To see the kids. Put together the Legos or construction set. Is that okay?"

Emotion tugged at Tasha's heart. During their marriage, Doug never did anything like this. And Blake and Libby were his biological kids. Brad, however, showered the kids with affection. His knack for entertaining them came in handy. When they were babies, Brad soothed Blake and Libby when they cried. Doug never bothered to try.

"Yes, the kids will be thrilled to see you. But you just got them something for their birthdays. Remember? You sent them those stuffed elephants. The green for Blake and a pink one for Libby. The things are big enough to ride. The toy hospital repaired Blake's a couple of times."

Brad nodded.

"I know. But I didn't—" He shook his head. "What do you mean, *toy hospital*?"

Tasha didn't think that was what Brad was going to say, but instead of asking him questions, she explained.

"The toy hospital is my parent's house. When their toys need fixing, they give them to my mom. She repairs everything. Stuffed elephants to wooden soldiers. She's talented."

As Brad turned onto her street, she glanced at the clock on the dashboard. The day flew by, which was a welcome surprise. Usually, time dragged with the kids in school. It was a nice feeling, despite her lack of accomplishments that day.

Brad parked in her driveway, and she hopped out. She opened the garage door as Brad's phone rang.

"I need to take this," said Brad looking at the caller ID.

"No problem," said Tasha. "Come on in when you're finished."

Once in the kitchen, Tasha put her purse on the counter and washed her hands. She pulled a glass down from the cabinet. She grabbed a second one, wondering if Brad might want something to drink, too. She filled the glasses with ice, then took lemonade and iced tea out of the fridge.

Brad opened the door, the two boxes under his arm. He smiled as she asked, "Would you like something to drink? This is your last chance to hydrate before Libby and Blake get home."

"I'd love an Arnold Palmer, thanks."

She nodded and poured both of them a glass. She handed it to him and took a seat at the kitchen table. Brad followed.

"So, Carlton's magic worked," Brad said, taking a sip. "You're moving without pain. How do you feel?"

"Like I never fell this morning. Never expected that could happen." Tasha sipped her drink as she gathered her thoughts. "How long can you stay this afternoon? It's best to give the kids a time frame so they know what to expect."

"I cleared my calendar for the afternoon. Uncle Brad is here to babysit."

The glass froze midway to her lips.

"Babysit? I don't need a babysitter."

"According to Carlton, you do. He thinks an afternoon to yourself would do you some good. I happen to have a free afternoon." His head tilted. "Are you questioning the advice of your chiropractor?"

Tasha put the glass on the table then leaned back in her seat.

"Okay. What is it with you and Carlton? Why are you both so concerned about me? I've never met the guy before. He works me into his schedule, then won't take payment. I've never heard of anyone doing that before."

Brad nodded.

"Well, Carlton's my friend and you're my family—" Brad held his hand up when she tried to interrupt. "He wants to help. Don't look a gift horse in the mouth."

"Understood, but I do have money to pay him. I won the lottery, remember?"

Smiling back at her Brad said, "How could I forget? Doug went on and on about it." The smile faded. "Speaking of my brother, I meant what I said in Sara's office. He can't tell me who I can and can't see."

She finished off her drink and frowned.

"I know that, but he can still make things difficult for me. Don't get me wrong, I appreciate your help today. But if he gets wind of this, both of us are going to hear about it."

Brad shrugged.

"Let him."

Before Tasha could respond, the kitchen door flew open. Blake and Libby rushed into the kitchen.

"Uncle Brad! I saw your truck! Why are you here?" Blake threw his arms around his uncle's leg.

Libby hugged his other leg. "Is everything all right? Daddy

said you couldn't come to visit us, so something must be wrong."

Great. Leave it to Libby to realize something is up as soon as she walked in the door.

Brad scooped both kids up for an upside-down hug. Laughter filled the room. Brad turned in circles a few times, then flipped both kids over and set them on the kitchen counter.

"Hello there to my favorite niece and nephew. How have you been? I haven't seen you in a while."

"We aren't allowed to sit on the counters." Libby squirmed to get off the counter.

"It's okay," said Tasha. "Uncle Brad didn't know."

Libby looked at her mother, then her uncle. Tasha thought her daughter was going to argue, but she changed tactics and tattled on her brother.

"I'm fine, but Blake is in trouble with Mrs. Anderson at school. Mrs. Anderson said he's too smart for his own good."

"That's what she used to say about me, and I turned out okay," said Brad.

Blake's mouth dropped open. "Mrs. Anderson was your teacher too? She must be really old, then!"

Brad laughed. "She isn't that old."

"Is everything all right?" Libby frowned. "Something's wrong. Daddy said Uncle Brad couldn't visit. Why is he here?"

"Libby, everything is fine. Uncle Brad can visit when he wants. He missed you and Blake. I ran into him today, so he came by to surprise you. That's it." Tasha looked at Brad over the kids' heads, hoping he would back her up.

"Yep, your mom and I ran into each other." Brad nodded back to Tasha. "And since I have a free afternoon, I offered to help you with homework so your mom could have the afternoon off."

"Mom doesn't have a job. How can she have an afternoon

off?" Blake noticed the box of Legos on the table. "Who are these for? Hey, that's my name. Is that for me?"

Tasha gave Brad credit. He distracted the kids to limit the number of questions asked.

It worked. Blake forgot his question and studied the box. He oohed and aahed over the figures included.

Libby saw the other box on the table, but she hesitated.

"Why do you need an afternoon off?" Tasha saw the moment when Libby realized what her uncle brought her. Libby didn't get excited about much, but her eyes lit up when she saw the engineering toy geared toward girls. Even then, she looked at her mom for an answer.

"It's nice to have time to yourself." Tasha nodded toward the table. "It's okay. You can go look at the toy."

With both kids examining their gifts, Brad smiled at Tasha.

"Commence your afternoon off." Brad smiled as the kids opened the boxes. "I have it under control."

"Yeah, you do. I'll have my phone if you need anything. Remember, homework first, then chores."

"Then we can play. Got it," said Brad. "We'll be fine."

Tasha admitted to herself he was right. Giving each kid a kiss on the top of their heads, she headed to her room to find some real shoes. She might as well take advantage of the free time. She didn't get much of it, and window-shopping without children was a luxury. The last thing she heard as she entered her bedroom was Libby.

"Thank you, Uncle Brad. This set is amazing. How did you know this is exactly what I wanted?"

10

"There's your minivan. Right where you left it," Helene said. She pulled her car into the parking spot next to Tasha's minivan. "Are you sure you don't want me to come shopping with you, honey? I'd be happy to. Your father's at car club. Tonight's their monthly dinner meeting so he won't miss me."

Tasha snorted.

"Mom, tonight is your Bunco group. No way you're missing that." Tasha dug the keys out of her purse. "I told you I'm fine. The fall wasn't that big of a deal, and I feel really good after Carlton's treatment." She leaned over and hugged her mother. "Brad is watching the kids. All is well. But thank you for driving me over here."

"You're welcome. It was the perfect opportunity to pump you for information." Tasha grimaced. Her mother never was subtle. "I'm still amazed Brad could get you in to see Dr. Reynolds so fast. I've tried for months, and his calendar is booked. Maybe you could ask Brad to work some magic for me."

"Okay, Mom. I'll get right on that. Good luck tonight at Bunco."

Helene glanced at her watch. "Well, if you insist. I'll just run by Betty's to pick up an apple pie for tonight's dessert. She saved me one."

Tasha stopped midway as she was sliding out of the car.

"Hey, remember you can't talk to anyone about this Dr. Purdue thing," said Tasha. "Not even with Betty."

"Betty already knows."

"Because you told her and you weren't supposed to. Promise me you won't mention it to anyone else."

Winking at her daughter, Helene said, "Fine. Pinky promise. I won't say a word. Now, close the door. If I want to get that pie, I have to get going."

Tasha got out of the car and closed the door. As Helene drove away, Tasha sighed. Her mother meant well, and she appreciated the ride to her minivan, but Helene liked to gossip with her friends, and Bunco was the perfect setting. Sara would have a field day if she knew Tasha sent her mother out in public with more gossip.

A prickling sensation ran down Tasha's neck, and she turned to face the building. Sure enough, Sara walked straight toward her. Tasha couldn't tell from the look on her sister's face what kind of mood she was in. Looking longingly at her mini-van, Tasha knew she had no choice but to find out.

"Hey. How was the rest of your day?" Maybe if she distracted Sara, she could get to the mall sooner.

"Why did Mom drop you off? Where's Brad?" Sara looked down at Tasha's feet. "Good. You changed shoes. Those slippers are dangerous."

Nodding in agreement, Tasha unlocked her minivan and put her purse inside. She leaned on the door, hoping her sister would take the hint.

"Carlton prescribed an afternoon at the mall, so Brad's

babysitting the kids. Mom had time before Bunco, so she drove me over here to pick up my minivan. Any other questions?"

Sara crossed her arms over her chest and frowned.

"Who is Carlton and how do you find someone to prescribe shopping?"

Tasha hid the smile that threatened. Apparently, she'd thrown her sister off. Sara didn't even blink when she heard her mother was headed to Bunco.

"Carlton is the chiropractor who fixed my back. He thinks I need to relax, so I'm going shopping," Tasha said. To tease her sister, she added, "Want to come with me? It would be fun."

Her sister let out a groan.

"You know it's a work day," said Sara. She looked at her watch. "And I have a call I need to get to."

"So why did you come out here? It's not like you haven't already seen me today."

Tasha saw her sister's shoulders rise, then fall. Something upset Sara. Then it dawned on Tasha what was bothering her sister.

"You're worried about me," said Tasha. From the look on her sister's face, she knew she was right. "You were worried I was actually hurt, weren't you? Admit it."

Sara tilted her head toward the office.

"Renee wouldn't stop talking about that woman with the concussion. It bothered me and when you didn't come back sooner to get your minivan, I wondered if something else happened. You are my sister. I'm allowed." Sara's eyes narrowed as she stared at Tasha. "But you look fine. And you're moving around like nothing happened. Did the chiropractor do that?"

Nodding, Tasha said, "Yep. It surprised me how fast he was able to fix me up. So, who am I to argue when he told me to take the afternoon off? Come with me. Reschedule your call."

Shaking her head, Sara said, "Not this one." She started

back toward the building before she turned and said, "You reminded Mom not to talk about Dr. Purdue, right?"

Tasha laughed as she got into the minivan.

"I did, but you know how well that works."

She closed the door, started the minivan, and backed out. Waving at Sara as she left the parking lot, Tasha headed to the shopping mall. She planned to enjoy the rest of the afternoon and worry about whatever her mother said at Bunco later.

11

The trip to the mall didn't disappoint. Free to wander from store to store, Tasha relished her freedom. She took her time, checking out whatever caught her interest. She passed the toy store in favor of a home accessories one. The candles and table decorations didn't suit her style, but she enjoyed browsing the aisles. Her mind wandered as she checked out the items for sale. Alone time was a rare commodity in her single parent life. She enjoyed the peace that came from indulging herself for a few minutes.

Back in the mall, a frilly dress in the display window of a girls clothing store caught her attention. Libby loved dressing up, so Tasha stepped in the store. As soon as she entered, she saw another dress. She reached out to feel the light pink fabric. When she touched the garment, the soft material glided through her fingertips. Unable to resist, Tasha picked up the dress and spun around with it.

Libby would love this! I would love this!

She continued to scour the racks, searching for hidden treasures. Tasha added a fun floral print shirt and a white, ruffly shirt to her "to buy" pile. She turned toward the cashier to pay when she heard a familiar voice from the past.

"Tasha? Is that you?"

It stopped her in her tracks. Her stomach clenched, and her shoulders tightened. She recognized the voice immediately, despite not having heard it in a month. How was it the one time she got to shop alone, she ran into her ex-husband?

Plastering a neutral look on her face, Tasha turned.

"Doug." Tasha nodded, struggling to suppress her surprise at her ex's appearance. Instead of the pressed, starched button-down shirt Doug usually wore, a wrinkled T-shirt hung loosely over his frame. Holes riddled the knees of his jeans, and his scuffed and frayed Cole Haan loafers finished the look.

He never looks like this. Something is wrong. That's the only reason he'd be here.

"What? You're not going to give me a welcome hug?" Doug threw out his arms. "I'm your husband, remember?"

"Ex-husband. I paid a lot of money for those two little letters."

Doug rewarded her with a combination laugh/cough.

"Still a smart ass, I see." Doug looked her up and down, then stopped his gaze on the pile of clothes over her arm. "Well, that's something new. Since when do you like to shop?"

"I shop all the time." Tasha redirected the conversation. "Why are you in town? You said it would be a cold day in hell before you came back here."

Doug stared at Tasha for a moment. She wasn't sure he was going to answer, but he finally shrugged.

"Business meeting. I'm here for a few days."

Based on his appearance, Tasha speculated business wasn't going well for him. She knew better than to voice her thoughts though. Instead, she asked a question he would never expect.

"Are you planning to see the kids? Blake is waiting for the Lego set you promised him," she said.

Doug grimaced as he brushed back overgrown bangs from his forehead. The movement struck Tasha as odd. He never let his hair grow that long.

"I never promised him a Lego set. I don't know why he would say something like that."

Tasha rolled her eyes. Arguing with her ex-husband was useless. A master at manipulating words, his selective memory was uncanny. She didn't bother to ask him if he wanted to see Libby. She knew the answer.

"Okay, then. I wish I could say it was nice to see you. It wasn't. So, I hope I don't see you later."

Her afternoon spoiled, Tasha turned to leave. She knew she was running away, but she didn't want to be near Doug. She wanted to be home with her kids.

"Natasha, wait a minute."

She froze as she realized he wasn't going to make leaving easy. Turning back, she glared at him.

"Why? What do you want?" Her hands shook under the clothes she held. "I don't have a lot of time."

Doug stared at the dress Tasha was holding.

"If you and that doctor hadn't screwed up, you wouldn't need to buy that frilly crap."

She glared at her ex-husband. "Just because you didn't get what you wanted doesn't mean you have to punish your daughter for it."

"I've told you before. She isn't my daughter. You and that doctor messed the whole thing up."

Tasha glanced around to see if anyone was listening to their conversation.

"Really? You want to discuss this in a public place? You seriously want to argue your daughter, the one conceived in a test tube because you had to have children at a specific time and place, is not yours?"

"I asked for two boys. Is it that difficult?" Doug's shoulders slumped, and he rubbed his hand through his hair. "That doctor guaranteed the babies' sex—"

"The doctor said he was confident but not certain, Doug. You got two healthy kids out of the deal. You don't have anything to complain about. You got what you were promised and didn't have to do any of the work."

"Oh right. You're never going to let that go, are you? Your body. The shots. The hormones. Blah, blah, blah." Doug made a face. "You know, we would have been just fine if you didn't complain so much."

She stared in disgust at the man she once planned to spend the rest of her life with.

"No, I think your girlfriend put an end to 'just fine'. I've gotta go. I need to get home."

"Wait a minute, Tasha. I need to talk to you. Why the hell else do you think I would be standing here?"

Tasha froze. She wanted to believe running into Doug was a coincidence, but he was right. There was no reason for him to be at the mall and even less reason to be in a store catering to young girl's clothing. Panic washed over her.

"You followed me here?" Her question came out as a shriek, and she glanced around to see if anyone noticed. "Why? What are you up to?"

"We need to talk." Doug ignored her questions. He glanced at the Rolex she got him the Christmas before he left her and the kids. "But not here. Let's go get some coffee. I have a proposition for you."

She bit her lip as she considered her options. Saying no to Doug wouldn't stop him from pestering her. He would show up again and again until he got what he wanted. Whether she liked it or not, Doug would always be part of her life because of Blake and Libby. She felt obligated to listen to him.

"I have to pay for these." Tasha nodded down at the clothes on her arm. "Where do you want to meet?"

"There's a coffee shop outside the store. Meet you there." Doug walked away without waiting for Tasha's agreement.

"Some things never change," Tasha muttered to herself and headed to the cashier.

12

Tasha scanned the coffee shop for Doug. She saw him hunched in the corner, engrossed in his phone. As she studied him, she frowned. His slouch was uncharacteristic. The gray streaks in his hair were new. Add the rumpled clothes to the equation, and Tasha knew something was wrong. The Doug she married never left the house unless he primped like a male model.

Something else occurred to her. It seemed awfully coincidental that Doug would show up the same week Dr. Purdue, the doctor he publicly humiliated on national television, sent Tasha a cease and desist letter.

I wonder what he did to upset Dr. Purdue this time.

Promising herself she would ask him, Tasha walked over.

"I'm here. What do you..." Tasha's voice trailed off when she noticed the second coffee cup on the table. She looked around, expecting to see China. "Where is she?"

"Where is who?"

Giving Doug her best evil eye, Tasha said, "China. Your girlfriend."

"Why would you assume China is here?"

Tasha nodded toward the second coffee cup.

"Isn't that hers?"

Doug shook his head.

"No. That's for you. It's a white chocolate mocha. With whipped cream. Your favorite. Or at least, it used to be."

Wary of his gesture, Tasha set her shopping bags down next to the table. She lowered herself into the seat across from him and picked up the cup and lifted off the lid. Sure enough, whipped cream covered the drink, forming a perfect dome.

Pressing the lid back on, she placed the cup on the table.

"Thank you."

Doug pursed his lips as he frowned.

"Aren't you going to drink it?"

Shaking her head, Tasha sat back in the chair.

"I'm not thirsty right now."

Doug's eyebrows shot up in surprise.

"You love coffee." He leaned forward and pushed the cup closer to her. "Go ahead. Drink some."

"What did you put in it? Arsenic? Cyanide? Antifreeze?" She didn't trust Doug. "You always wanted to get rid of me."

Doug rolled his eyes.

"I didn't poison your coffee. I'm trying to be nice." He picked up the cup, gulped down the hot liquid, then held the cup out to her. "See? It's fine."

Tasha's mouth watered at the smell of the fresh coffee, but she kept her arms crossed over her chest. She stared wistfully at the coffee cup as she said, "Great. Now, it's got your germs on it."

"And you call me childish." Doug sipped his own coffee. "Don't you want to tell me how Blake is? Or how your love life is going? I thought you liked a little chitchat before getting down to business."

"I'm not in the chitchat mood. If you bothered to call Blake, you'd know how he was," Tasha snapped. "And what about Libby? Aren't you even curious about her?"

Doug shrugged.

"Not really." He took another sip of his coffee. "You didn't mention your love life. That going so well you don't feel the need to discuss it?"

He's trying to aggravate me. That's what he does. Do not react. Let him say his piece and then I'm out of here. After I get coffee.

"What do you want, Doug?" she asked, eyeing the coffee. "Some of us have things to do."

"Fine. If you want to skip the pleasantries, I have a business proposal for you."

Tasha's eyes flew from the coffee cup to her ex-husband's face. The wry smile she fell in love with appeared, and his eyes lit up. She realized what he was doing.

He's trying to charm me. Guard up, Tasha.

"Ahh. Glad to see I have your attention."

The sarcasm hammered another nail in her resolve to resist this man. He wasn't who she thought he was. Even when their marriage was good, Doug never shared his business matters with her. It irritated her, but she let it go. She let a lot of things go. It was his affair with the trampy real estate agent that jolted her out of her idyllic existence.

Before she realized what she was doing, Tasha reached for the cup of coffee. She took a sip and sighed as the hot liquid slid down her throat. Doug smiled.

"Didn't expect that, did you?" His voice softened, and Tasha saw more of the old Doug in the current disheveled one. "I am a nice guy, remember?"

Something niggled at the back of her mind. Anytime Doug wanted something from her, he always gave her a gift. Usually, it was flowers or jewelry. Looking at the coffee in her hand, she realized Doug was manipulating her like he did before. Whatever this proposal was, he needed her help with it. He thought if he turned on the charm—or in this case the coffee—she'd fall for it.

Embarrassment for repeating the same pattern of her married life made her hand tremble. She wasn't that person anymore. No way would she fall into the same trap again. Tasha leaned forward to set the coffee cup on the table. She didn't want any part of Doug's bribes. As she pulled back, her shaking hand knocked the cup to the floor, splattering coffee as it went. Wet spots appeared on Doug's jeans and shoes.

Tasha tensed as she reached for some napkins. She knew what would happen next. Doug would rant and complain about her clumsiness.

Instead, he waved to a barista who came over with a towel and helped get the liquid cleaned up. Despite her protests, the barista took the cup back for a refill.

Tasha wiped at the coffee spots on her own pants as she said, "I'm sorry. That was an accident."

"I know." He shrugged. "It might be my fault. I surprised you."

Startled by Doug's reaction, she frowned.

"You're not going to yell at me?"

"What good is that going to do?" Doug grabbed a few napkins and dabbed at the spots on his shirt. "What's done is done."

Staring at her ex-husband, Tasha didn't know what to say. Two times in a row, he surprised her with compassion she didn't know he had. The old Doug would have yelled and screamed about how clumsy she was. He would have accused her of spilling the coffee on purpose. She didn't know how to comprehend the new Doug.

If he's making an effort, maybe I should too.

"You said you have a business proposal for me. What is it?"

She watched his face for signs of manipulation. He met her gaze straight on, something he never used to do. The suspicion she felt died down as he leaned forward.

"It's a great opportunity. It would be good for both you and the kids."

13

Tasha let her coffee go cold while Doug explained the opportunity.

"This town doesn't have any children's entertainment centers. You complained all the time the kids didn't have anything to do in the winter months. They were bored when they couldn't go outside," Doug said. "Opening an indoor inflatable center and trampoline park would give them something to do."

She started to interrupt, but Doug pulled a rumpled pamphlet from his back pocket and tossed it on the table. Tasha picked it up as he continued talking.

"Here's the business plan. It's a franchise opportunity. It can't fail. All you need to do is write a check for $150,000, and I'll take care of the rest."

Tasha glanced up at Doug, then returned her gaze to the brochure. She flipped through it until she made her way to the financial investment part. Sure enough, the capital required to open the business was exactly $150,000.

She dropped the brochure on the table and sat back in the chair. Crossing her arms over her chest, Tasha debated how to handle the situation. The idea of having something to do during the day was appealing. The kids loved running through obstacle courses and racing down giant slides. But she didn't know what to make of Doug's sudden interest in his children or his appearance in town.

Tasha needed more information.

"So, you want me to pay for a business that you're going to run?"

Doug nodded. A smile brightened his face.

"Exactly. I knew this would make sense to you. The kids will love it."

She held up her hand.

"Hold on. Why don't you invest some of your own money in this? Last I recall you walked away with, oh I don't know, roughly $50 million in the divorce. Use some of that and I'll bring the kids to the park to visit. But that's only if China tells me she's okay with this."

Doug's smile dimmed, and Tasha thought his face paled.

"You'd be a silent partner." He grabbed the pamphlet back from the table. "I'll get the location and hire employees. You don't have any business experience, anyway. This is right up my alley."

Aware of the fact he didn't answer the money question, Tasha tried a different tactic.

"Where did you plan to be when you run this business?"

A sense of foreboding knotted Tasha's stomach when he didn't answer immediately, and Tasha knew her answer.

"You're going back to St. Thomas, aren't you? You want me to front the money on this and take all the risk, while you sit on the beach and cash the checks. That's exactly what you're up to."

She watched as more color drained from Doug's face. Add the pale face with the sneer of irritation she knew so well, Tasha prepared herself for whatever insult Doug flung next.

"Why do you always have to make things so difficult? This is for you and the kids."

Tasha shrugged.

"I can take the kids to a bounce house. I don't need to own one. You need to come clean with me. What is this all about?" she asked. Tasha pointed at him as she spoke. "Your loafers are scuffed, and your clothes are wrinkled. I've never seen your hair that long before." Her eyes widened when the truth dawned on her. "You're broke. You lost all that money. Didn't you?"

Instead of confirming her suspicion, Doug cleared his throat and folded the pamphlet.

"Why do you always have to be so negative? I'm including you and the kids in a once-in-a-lifetime opportunity, and you sit there making accusations."

"I'm not accusing you of anything. I asked a question." Tasha leaned forward and looked Doug in the eye. "Did you lose the money?"

Instead of answering, Doug continued to extol the virtues of owning a business. He ranted on about how good a bounce house would be for the kids and Tasha found herself fighting off guilt. She wanted to be the best mom she could be. She'd planned to have the happiest family possible. Instead, she got Doug and the chaos that came in the wake of all his stupid ideas.

The problem was she still let him control her. He did it well. He knew the kids were her kryptonite, and Doug planned to use them against her.

It's like we never got divorced. What I am I doing here?

She inhaled a few deep breaths to calm herself. If she learned nothing else from their marriage, she knew she couldn't say no to Doug and expect to walk away without a fight. This was another of Doug's schemes. She'd lived through them before, like the multi-level marketing company which sold health supplements made of sawdust. The bounce house idea seemed legitimate, but that didn't mean anything. Sure, the kids would love it and it might make money, but she'd never see a penny. Knowing Doug, she wouldn't get her investment back, either.

She tuned back in to the conversation as Doug said, "Tasha, this one can work. Once this one is up and running, I can scout around for another location. Plus, the kids could work there when they got older. A family business."

Rather than argue with him, Tasha decided to stall him. She shrugged with what she hoped was an "I don't have a care in the world" attitude and said, "Fine. I'll think about it." She picked up her purse and pulled out her cell phone. "Let me take a picture of the brochure. I want Sara to look into it first."

She stopped what she was doing when she saw a look of smug satisfaction cross Doug's face.

"This does not mean I agree to do this. It means I will investigate the opportunity," said Tasha. "Don't get any bright ideas."

A smile filled Doug's face.

"You won't be disappointed. I promise."

14

T asha's shoulders slumped as she turned her minivan off in the garage. The entire ride home from the mall she analyzed the conversation with Doug. While she'd pushed back more today than she had in the past, she still told him she'd think about his asinine offer.

"Why didn't I tell him no and be done with it?" she asked herself as she thumped her head against the steering wheel. A wave of shame washed over her. She didn't want to participate in his business plan. And now she had to talk to Doug again so she could tell him what she should have told him already.

"Oh my God. I'm such an idiot," she said. Her words echoed in the empty minivan. "I played right into his hands. Why do I let him do this to me? I should be stronger than this."

Aware that the kids or Brad might investigate why she was sitting in her minivan, she rubbed her hands over her face.

"Pull yourself together, Natasha. You did this to yourself. You're going to have to undo it."

She pulled herself and her shopping bags out of the minivan and trudged to the door leading into the kitchen. When she reached out to open it, she took a deep breath. She refused to take her bad mood inside the house. Hopefully, the kids had had a good time with Uncle Brad. They didn't deserve to have their evening ruined because their mother couldn't say no to her ex-husband.

Satisfied she looked calm and collected, Tasha opened the door. The smell of chocolate chip cookies surrounded her. Laughter and footsteps beckoned her inside. The tension in her shoulders released, and she pushed Doug to the back of her mind.

She walked into the kitchen. A plate of fresh cookies greeted her from the counter. The kitchen was sparkling clean, which made her smile. Whenever she baked, the kitchen was a mess.

"Mommy!" Blake and Libby screamed in unison when they ran into the room.

"Uncle Brad let us play tag inside, and we built a fort." Blake raised his arm. "I won tag!"

"He also rolled us up in the carpet so we could be butter-flies." Libby rolled her eyes at her brother. "And we made cookies!"

"When can he come back?" asked Blake.

Tasha smiled at the sight of the twins. Their clothes were rumpled. Both of their faces were flushed from rushing around, and Libby's hair was messy and tangled. It had been a long time since she'd seen either of them so excited.

"The kitchen is so clean. Are you sure you made cookies?" teased Tasha.

"Blake and Libby cleaned up the kitchen after we baked." Brad walked into the kitchen. "We made a deal. They could only eat the cookies if they cleaned up the kitchen. You should have told me Libby was a good sweeper. I may need her to clean my house."

Blake stood up straighter. "I helped, too. I wiped cabinets and put dishes away."

"You did great, buddy. Don't forget, you dried the dishes."

Tasha was pleased they'd helped Brad. They did their chores, but it was good for them to work with other adults. Brad's compliments were important for the kids. They were proud of the work they'd done.

"Do you want to taste a cookie, Mommy?" Libby pointed to the plate. "We made chocolate chip. Uncle Brad used Grandma's recipe."

"They're fluffy like Grandma's." Blake grabbed a cookie from the plate. "Not like when we make them. Flat and crunchy."

Curious, Tasha took the cookie Blake offered her. One bite told her all she needed to know. The cookies were as good as her mother's.

"How did you do it?" Tasha took another bite. "Mine never turn out like this."

Brad shrugged. "Guess we got lucky, guys. Your grandma's cookies are hard to beat. I bet your mom's are good, too."

Blake shook his head. "No, hers are crunchy."

"But they still taste good." Libby grabbed Tasha's hand and squeezed it. Tasha grinned down at her daughter. Leave it to Libby to pick up on the fact she was sensitive about the quality of her cookies.

Tasha changed the subject to steer clear of the great cookie debate. "Did you have time to get homework done, or was it just butterflies and cookies all afternoon?" She was glad to see the kids having so much fun, but it was a school night.

"Finished." Libby always finished homework, so Tasha wasn't surprised. She worried about Blake. He hated doing his and got upset anytime the subject of homework came up.

"Done. Uncle Brad checked it and helped me fix my mistakes," said Blake. "And I read to him."

Brad looked at Tasha with a sheepish grin.

"I told the kids we couldn't play until they finished their

homework. I brought some paperwork in from the truck, so we all did our work together."

Tasha gazed from Brad to Blake and back to Brad. She wasn't sure what to say. Homework time was usually filled with tears and tantrums, not butterflies and cookies. Even when she did sit down with Blake, it didn't work out the way it did for Brad.

Disgusted at herself for feeling jealous, she pasted a big smile on her face.

"Well, I'm glad everyone got their work done. I imagine Uncle Brad needs to get back to work." Tasha looked at the clock. "Or to dinner. Make sure you thank him for the cookies and help with your homework."

"Can Uncle Brad stay for dinner? Please! We could order a pizza," said Blake.

For once, Libby agreed with her brother.

"Yeah, we should do something nice for Uncle Brad, since he was so nice to us today."

"You don't need to do anything nice for me, guys. I like to help. I haven't been able to hang out with you for a while, and today was great. I had a good time making cookies and playing, but your mom's right." Brad looked at Tasha and nodded. "I have to get to work. I have a dinner meeting. That's what my homework was. Those papers are for my next project."

"When can we see you again, Uncle Brad?" said Libby.

"Can you come to my soccer game?" Blake asked.

Libby frowned. "What about my piano recital?"

"Guys, Uncle Brad is busy. He had some time today, but we can't expect him to come to all our activities," said Tasha. "He's a busy architect, remember?"

She expected the kids to start begging, but they didn't. They stood there, looking at their uncle. Tasha turned to Brad to see why the kids were staring. A big smile plastered itself across Brad's face.

"Actually, I'd love to come to a soccer game and a piano recital," he said, pulling his phone from his pocket. "Do you have the dates? I'll put them into my calendar right now."

Libby and Blake threw themselves at Brad, giving him hugs and kisses. Tasha watched from where she stood. Sadness poured over her as she watched the scene in front of her.

This is what our life was supposed to be like.

"The schedules are in my office. I'll go get them. Be right back."

She hustled to her office before anyone could respond. Tasha grabbed the schedules from her corkboard. She leaned against the door and closed her eyes as she gave herself a mental lashing.

Get a grip. Life's not perfect, but Blake and Libby are happy. The problem is you, Natasha. They're happy so why can't you be too?

Knowing she didn't have time for more self-deprecation, Tasha walked back to the kitchen. On the floor, the kids were sitting on Brad's lap. Steeling herself for the next wave of guilt, she thrust out the schedules to Brad.

"Here," she said handing over the documents. "Libby. Blake. Let Uncle Brad up off the floor. He needs to get going to his meeting, and we don't want to make him late."

"Okay, but he should take some cookies," Libby said as she hopped off the floor. "He might get hungry during his meeting."

She headed to the pantry, and Blake ran after her.

Tasha watched as Brad entered the dates into his phone.

"Thanks for doing all this. You didn't need to go to all the trouble, but the kids had fun. You know, it's okay if you can't come to the game or recital. I can explain to the kids you're busy."

"I wouldn't have offered if I didn't mean it." Brad stood up and looked at her. He frowned as he said, "Something happened at the mall, didn't it?"

She shook her head.

"I spent more money than I needed to, but other than that, I'm fine."

Brad glanced toward the pantry when he heard Blake and Libby arguing. Tasha started toward the door when Brad took her arm.

"Let them work it out on their own," he said. "Stay here and tell me what's wrong. You left here happy and relaxed. Right before you left to get the soccer schedule, I thought you were going to burst out crying. What happened?"

Tasha crossed her arms over her chest. She leaned against the wall.

He's trying to help. Brad isn't going to judge you for being a wimp around Doug.

Letting out a long sigh, she said, "I ran into Doug at the mall. He wants me to go into business with him."

Tasha's first instinct was to laugh at the shocked expression on Brad's face, but she caught herself.

"You said no, didn't you?" Brad asked. When she didn't answer immediately, he said, "What did you agree to?"

Without looking at his face, she said, "I didn't agree to anything. I took the information, and I plan to tell him no."

"But you beat yourself up because you didn't tell him to go to hell right then and there, didn't you?" Brad mimicked Tasha as he crossed his arms. "Which also explains why you ran out of the room a minute ago. Tasha, you never did anything wrong, so don't let him convince you otherwise. I know he's my brother, but I don't stand behind his choices."

Before Tasha could respond, Libby and Blake rushed out of the pantry and grabbed Brad's hands. They walked him to the front door, then Libby handed him a bag of cookies. Brad crouched down to give each of them a hug.

Tasha pasted a smile on her face as she watched the three of them together.

This is better than nothing. You have to admit that.

"Mommy, you need to say goodbye, too!" Libby exclaimed.

Blake agreed with his sister. "Yeah. And tell Uncle Brad thank you for babysitting us."

A genuine smile stretched across her cheeks.

"You're right, guys. I do need to say thank you."

Without warning, Brad wrapped Tasha in a bear hug. He whispered in her ear, "Call me if you need help with Doug. But I know you can stand up to him. Trust yourself."

He let her go and waved to everyone.

"I'll see you at the soccer game and the piano recital," he said as he let himself out the door. With a backward glance, he said to Tasha, "Why don't you give your sister a call? I bet she has some words of wisdom."

As the door closed, Tasha turned back to her kids.

"Can we have another cookie?" asked Blake.

"No, honey. It's time for dinner," said Tasha. "But you can have one for dessert. Let's go get dinner ready."

As the three of them headed to the kitchen, Tasha couldn't help but wonder what her sister would say if she called. Maybe she'd find out later. But for now, feeding her children took priority.

15

Sara breathed a sigh of relief as she stretched her arms over her head. Her day had been anything but normal. While her sister and the pig slipper incident ended up being benign, dealing with her latest client left Sara with the start of a tension headache. Her client thought he could dissolve his marriage through mediation, but his partner wasn't cooperating. Instead of a few months of mediation, the divorce could take years. That was lucrative for the law firm, but it made Sara sad.

"Another good reason for a prenup," Sara said under her breath as she reached for the file Tasha dropped off. She wanted to investigate Dr. Purdue's allegations before she left the office for yoga class.

The thought of her Wednesday night class made her smile. Not because she liked sweating buckets for ninety minutes, though she did like the way her body was more toned than it had been in years.

No, Sara wanted to see the guy in the front row with the midnight-blue mat and the fluorescent-green yoga shorts. Lately, yoga night doubled as date night for Sara. Even though she didn't know Yoga Guy's name, her imaginary conversations with him were plentiful. Sara imagined telling him about Tasha's latest predicament. Yoga Guy, or Guy as she called him in her mind, would agree the entire situation was disheartening.

"It's a shame doctors sue their own patients these days. Everyone is so litigious." He would smile up at her from Downward Facing Dog. "No offense to the lawyers in the room."

Sara frowned. Yoga Guy didn't know she was a lawyer. Hell, he didn't even know her name. But he was right, or at least her imagination was. It was sad that everyone sued each other for no reason at all.

"Well, not for no reason," Sara said after she read through Dr. Purdue's letter to Tasha. The doctor included examples of the negative reviews and accusations Tasha allegedly made against him. Frowning, Sara wondered if her sister really had posted a review and forgot about it. Sara turned back to her computer and pulled up the first website on Purdue's list.

She entered the doctor's name in the search bar and hit enter. Grabbing her ever-present water bottle, she leaned back to take a sip, before checking out the search results. It took her less than a minute to figure out what irked Dr. Purdue and caused him to retaliate against the client testimonials.

Negative and one-star reviews dominated his page. Sara scanned the comments. After reading a dozen of them, she noted they all sounded similar. A glance at the names of the reviewers, though, made her laugh out loud. Each review listed a famous artist, writer, and musician as its author.

"Shakespeare died in 1616," she said to herself. "He most definitely did not review an infertility doctor."

Now that she had an inkling of what was happening, Sara doubted the validity of these reviews. She continued down the list, making note of what could be a real name here and there.

It wasn't until she reached the last page of the list when she noticed a familiar name, Natasha Gerome.

"Damn it." She clicked on the link to read the full review. Sure enough, the verbiage was like the words Cicero, Van Gogh, and Plato wrote in their reviews of Dr. Purdue. Someone wanted to tank Dr. Purdue's reputation and seemed to be having fun in the process. Sara's money was on Doug.

Looking at the list of names she wrote down, an idea formed. She pulled up her favorite social media application and typed in the names from her list. Sara located about half of the families online and scrolled through their profiles. Sure enough, all had children under the age of ten. Sara pushed back from her desk and stood up. She needed to walk around. It helped her think as she considered the possibilities.

Someone was mixing real patient reviews in with fake ones. Was Doug smart enough to set Tasha up like this? Sara didn't think so, but she didn't know for sure. She'd never taken the time to get to know him. She hated him from the first time they met.

Picking up the miniature rake for her Zen garden, Sara drew lines in the sand as she remembered when Tasha introduced her to Doug. He'd been dressed impeccably, not a hair out of place. His manners were polite, but something hadn't seemed right. No one was that pulled together, which is what made Sara doubt his authenticity. Then, he made a pass at her a few weeks after he and Tasha started dating. She knew she did the right thing by warning her sister, but Sara cringed when she remembered Tasha's reaction.

"You're jealous you couldn't get a guy like this. You always thought you were better than me, didn't you?" Sara closed her eyes as the image of Tasha's face popped into her mind. "You may be older than me and smarter than me, but that doesn't mean I'm not a good judge of character."

"I'm not saying that, Tasha. I think the guy is weird. I don't want you getting taken advantage of," Sara recalled the look on her sister's face. "What? You don't believe there's anything wrong with this guy?"

"No, I don't. You're mad I have a boyfriend. You made up this ridiculous story about him so I'd stop seeing him and you could date him. Well, it's not going to work. He's a great guy so leave us alone."

She dropped the rake back in the garden and turned back to her desk. It didn't change anything to wonder what would have happened if she had kept her mouth shut. Maybe Tasha would have realized sooner what a loser Doug was and left him. Instead, Doug left her for another woman. Sara's attempt to help had hurt their relationship but didn't get rid of Doug.

"Not this time," Sara muttered and sat back down at her desk. She would figure out what Doug was up to. She wasn't going to let the asshole screw up her relationship with her sister anymore. It was up to her to prove that Doug used Tasha's name to review Dr. Purdue.

Half an hour later, her phone rang. She checked the clock to make sure she had time for the call, then grabbed the phone without checking caller ID.

"Sara Shaw speaking."

"Hey. It's me." Tasha's voice sounded tired. "Do you have a minute?"

"I do, but just that. I'm finishing up some work, then heading out."

No need to tell her what I'm working on yet. Once I have more details, I'll update her.

"Okay. This will only take a minute. I wasn't going to call you, but Brad thought it would be a good idea."

Sara sat up straight when she heard Brad's name.

"Are you hurt? I knew you hit the ground hard this morning. I should have taken you to the hospital myself."

She heard the irritation in her sister's voice when she spoke.

"I'm fine. The trip to the chiropractor fixed everything. And the prescribed shopping trip was nice," Tasha paused before adding, "for the most part."

"What's that supposed to mean?"

Tasha cleared her throat and said, "Doug showed up at the mall today."

"What?" Sara was thankful it was after hours as her voice came out as a screech. "What did he want? Are you okay?"

"I'm fine. At least, I'm better than he is. He looked terrible, Sara. I think he's broke."

Sara snorted.

"That's impossible. How could anyone go through $58 million in a couple of years?"

"Leave it to you to remember exactly how much money he got. I don't know, but he asked me for money. He wants $150,000 for start-up costs in a business."

Putting her head in her hand, Sara closed her eyes and asked, "What did you tell him?" She knew this call took a lot of effort on Tasha's part and she didn't want to shut her down. Her mother would be proud of her. If she ever told her. Which she didn't plan on doing. "Did you give him any money?"

She heard her sister let out a long breath before answering.

"I wanted to tell him no. I really did. But I was afraid I'd make him mad if I gave him an answer right away, so I stalled." Tasha sniffled, as if she'd been crying over the matter. "I told him I needed to run it past you."

Sara lifted her head up in shock her sister would turn to her. It was a big deal for her to call yesterday about the Purdue matter, but this was closer to home. Maybe they were closer than she thought.

"You aren't married to him anymore. There isn't anything he can do if you tell him no. And you know I'm going to say no to anything that sleaze ball asks for." When Tasha didn't answer, Sara asked, "What are you really worried about?"

"I was doing okay, Sara. Not great. But okay. He ruined our lives and then he left. And I got over it. I got stronger. But the second I see him, I revert back to how I used to be." Sara heard the tears in her sister's voice. "I don't have the energy for this. Plus the whole mess with Dr. Purdue. I freaked out."

Clicking her computer screen back to life, Sara decided now was the time to give her sister an update. Tasha needed something else to focus on aside from her dubious ex-husband.

"Speaking of Dr. Purdue, I did some research on his claims. It looks like someone is posting fake reviews using other people's names. Yours happens to be one of them."

"Great. What do we do now?"

"Leave that to me. Prepare yourself to tell Doug no when he calls you back. I'll keep looking into the Purdue issue." She hesitated before adding, "I'll help you figure this out, okay?"

"Okay. Thank you."

Sara put the phone back on the hook before looking at the clock on her computer. Crap. She needed to leave for yoga, and she hadn't finished her research on Purdue. Gathering her files, she put them and her laptop into her briefcase. It would have to wait until later. Then she would figure out what Doug was up to.

16

"So, does Sara have any insight about this mess with Dr. Purdue?" Tasha's mom unloaded a bag of vegetables and put them on the counter. "If you ask me, Doug's behind this mess. 100%. This is something he would do. I can't understand how his parents raised him to behave like this. And how Brad turned out so nice."

Tasha began washing vegetables. This was a repeat of the conversation they had many times over the years, and Tasha knew her mother wasn't finished yet.

"I can't imagine how disappointed Roger and Eveline were when Doug left you. She stopped coming to Bunco, mah-jong, and wine tasting."

Taking her cue, Tasha said, "I hear she still goes to bridge club. You could always go there if you want to talk to her."

Tasha smiled at the look of irritation on Helene's face.

"I know what you're doing, young lady. You might think it's funny I'm not invited to play bridge anymore. Completely unfair. I had no way of knowing Mildred was allergic to coconuts when I brought ambrosia salad. She should have told someone."

"Be glad she carried one of those epinephrine things. Otherwise, you'd have been kicked out of more than bridge club." Tasha scrubbed the dirt off the carrots and decided she'd teased her mother enough. "Anyway, yes, she thinks she may have a lead."

Helene peeled the carrots Tasha just washed.

"Do I get more details than that?"

"When I have some. Really, that's all she's told me. She gave me some advice about Doug." As soon as the words came out of her mouth, Tasha knew she'd said too much.

Sure enough, the vegetable peeler came to a halt.

"Why do you need advice about Doug? I thought he was ignoring you from St. Thomas." Helene picked up the peeler again and groused, "What kind of father intentionally ignores his own children? I don't understand."

Tasha knew she needed to tell Helene about the run-in with Doug, but she didn't want to discuss it right now.

"The usual stuff, really. I shouldn't agree to anything Doug says. If I were to run into him, I mean." Tasha turned to the sink to wash the rest of the vegetables. "You can't say anything, either. I already owe Betty new uniforms for the softball team because of your conversation."

"My conversation about what?" Helene pretended she didn't know what Tasha was talking about. "How did the babysitting go with Brad? He always was such a nice boy. He misses the kids, and they miss him."

Relieved to discuss something else, Tasha said, "The kids had a great time. They baked your chocolate chip cookies. And get this. Blake said they're as good as yours."

Helene's already perfect posture straightened more than Tasha thought possible. "There is no way someone else's cookies are as good as mine. Especially a man's."

Tasha walked to the cookie jar and got one for her mother.

"Taste one and see."

Helene bit into the cookie. Her eyes opened wide as she chewed it. She swallowed and shook her head.

"Well, I'll be. He did well. I don't think they're as fluffy as mine, but they are better than those flat disks you call cookies." Helene brushed the crumbs off her hands and went back to the carrots.

Tasha was surprised her mother gave Brad credit but was glad she wasn't upset about it. Helene would be mad enough when she told her about running into Doug the previous afternoon. Taking a deep breath, she started to tell her mother about her impromptu coffee when Helene asked her a question.

"Have you decided what you're doing with your free Saturday evening?"

"No." Tasha was immediately on guard. Her mother rarely asked what she was doing when the kids spent the night, so she knew something was up. She hoped she was wrong, but Tasha knew her mother. "Just thought I would drop the kids off and come home to a quiet house."

"That's what I thought. Good thing I'm around to take care of you." Helene wiped her hands on a kitchen towel and walked to her purse. She dug out a card. "I RSVP'd you to this."

Glancing at the card, Tasha rolled her eyes.

"Mother, this is an invitation to a speed dating group."

"I'm so glad you can read," said Helene. "Now, let's see how you do at dating."

"Where did you get this? No, don't answer that. I don't want to know. Better question—how long have you known about this?"

Helene shrugged. "A week or so. I thought I'd surprise you."

"Mission accomplished. Why did you do this? Isn't my life complicated enough as it is?"

"Sweetie, I had no idea you were going to get yourself mixed up in a scandal with that Dr. Purdue."

"It's not a scandal, Mom. More of a misunderstanding."

Rolling her eyes, Helene said, "Well, whatever it was, had I known you were going to needlessly complicate your life this week, I would have held off on speed dating until next month." Helene returned to the carrots. "As it is, you already have a sitter for Saturday night, so you might as well go."

Tasha pondered her mother's words as they finished the vegetables in companionable silence. Her mom was right as usual. The kids would be fine, and she had nothing else to do. She was going to reserve judgment of speed dating though. Her luck with men couldn't get any worse, could it?

17

Libby and Blake chowed down on the special Friday-morning breakfast Tasha made. Once a week, Tasha fixed something more than the normal weekday cereal. Today's treat was eggs Benedict.

Tasha watched them eat as she sipped her cup of tea. She wanted to call Sara to find out what was going on with Dr. Purdue, but she knew bothering Sara before she was ready to talk only made her grumpy. She didn't want to wait too long though.

Since she couldn't call, she turned her focus on whether she was going to the speed dating session tomorrow night. Her mother meant well, but Helene didn't realize how Tasha felt about dating, that she was embarrassed her best prospect for love was due to her mother.

"Why are you worried, Mommy?" Libby finished off her breakfast.

"Why do you think I'm worried?"

Libby shrugged. "You have a frown. And you made us eggs with sauce from that cooking magazine you hate."

"I'm not frowning, and I don't hate it. It's just got some challenging recipes." Tasha tried to relax her facial muscles. This was one of those times when Botox would come in handy. No wrinkles and no frowns.

Libby was right though. She was worried, and she didn't hide it well. Tasha should have canceled Saturday night. She would be better off at home, ordering Chinese, drinking a glass of wine, and watching some mindless reality TV show. Instead, she would be at a hotel, eating cold buffet food, and drinking a glass of bad wine with a bunch of strangers who belonged on a mindless reality TV show.

"Is Uncle Brad coming to my soccer game?" mumbled Blake through a mouthful of food. "Or is he going to cancel like Daddy does because China doesn't want to come?"

Tasha drew in a quick breath. She had no idea Blake knew why Doug never made it to soccer games. Doug came by himself once but missed China so much, he left early. He never offered to come to another game, and Tasha didn't bother to give him the latest schedule.

"How do you know China doesn't want to come?" Tasha asked Blake.

"Because Grandma said China probably liked Jell-O wrestling better." Libby drank the last of her milk. "She said it was shallow and cheap, just like she was."

Tasha choked. She needed to talk to her mom. Tasha couldn't argue with her mother's logic but repeating it to Blake and Libby wasn't a good idea.

"We know." Libby read her mom's mind. "Grandma said we can't say this to Daddy or China. She said it would be rude."

"Then why did she say it, I wonder?" Tasha was curious if her mother gave herself an escape clause.

"Grandma said it was the truth, and you can't argue with the truth." Finished talking about his grandmother, Blake asked again, "Is Uncle Brad coming to my soccer game?"

"He put it in his calendar, Blake," Tasha said. "I'm sure he'll try, but don't be disappointed if he can't make it."

"I bet he does. He always keeps his promises." Libby spun herself around in the center of the kitchen. "He'll come to my piano recital. I know he will."

"Why would he come to a stupid piano recital?" Blake asked to agitate his sister. "No one wants to go to those."

"Uncle Brad does want to come," yelled Libby, clearly upset. "Uncle Brad doesn't lie like Daddy. If he says he will come, he will."

Tasha waited to see how Blake would respond before she mediated the argument.

Blake took a moment to think. "You're right. Uncle Brad will be there. Even for a stupid recital."

Satisfied with her brother's response, Libby took her empty dish to the sink.

"Olivia's counselor told her parents never mean to hurt their children, but they do because sometimes adults are just big children themselves," said Libby.

"Who is Olivia, and why is she seeing a counselor?" The abrupt change of subject confused Tasha.

"She's the new girl in my class. I don't know why she sees a counselor, but she has a nanny, and a driver, and a cook."

"Her twin brother, Oliver, is in my class." Blake wiped his face with his sleeve. "He said his mom fell in love with her spin instructor, and they're having an affair."

Tasha decided to ignore the affair.

"What about Oliver and Olivia's dad?" Tasha resisted asking who in their right minds would name fraternal twins Oliver and Olivia, but she didn't want to confuse the discussion.

"He has a boyfriend named Mr. Robert." Libby grabbed her backpack. "Mr. Robert has a dog named Tiny. Olivia said she likes the dog, but the boyfriend isn't very nice. Mr. Robert's a vegan and won't let her eat junk food."

"Well, that's nice he wants her to eat food that's good for her." Tasha made a mental note to attend the next PTO meeting so she could catch up on who was still married and who was dating. It would make these breakfast conversations easier.

Blake left his empty plate on the table and went to get his backpack.

"But, Mom, the stuff Oliver brings in his lunch is gross. He had a packet of worms yesterday because he said they're high in protein."

"Worms are animals. Vegans don't eat animals, Blake." Tasha smiled before she continued. "I can think of worse things to eat than worms."

"It was seaweed that looked like worms," Libby said, interrupting her mother. "It was stringy and crunchy. I tasted some of Olivia's. It was good."

Leave it to Libby to find something positive to say about seaweed. Tasha silently agreed with Blake—seaweed looked like worms. A quick glance at the clock told Tasha it was bus time.

"Everyone, time to go. Do you have backpacks? Lunches? A hug from me?" Tasha went through the morning checklist and gave each of her kids a bear hug. She rushed them out the door as the bus pulled up. She watched them get on and waved goodbye.

Heading back into the kitchen, Tasha began the clean-up process. She hated cleaning up more than cooking, but it was part of the deal. To eat, you must cook. To cook, you must clean. Tasha thought she should design a cute little kitchen plaque with those sayings just for the fun of it. And if that didn't keep her mind occupied while she waited for Sara, Tasha could contemplate what to wear to speed dating. That was about as depressing as the dishes.

18

S ara rearranged the papers in Tasha's file. The package
Tasha dropped off on Wednesday contained everything
she needed, but not in the tidy fashion Sara liked.
Rather than letting Renee handle the documents, Sara did it
herself. She knew it wasn't a good use of her time, but it let her
go through all the information again.

Plus, organizing relaxed her.

Sara knew her sister wasn't neat, but she was grateful Tasha
kept her paperwork in one place. "And she had the sense to
make copies of everything," mumbled she to herself.

"Who made copies?" Bill stuck his head into Sara's office.
"Copies of what?"

Sara closed the last fastener in the file and looked up at her
partner. She shook her head slightly.

"The trouble with partners," said Sara teasingly, "is they're
never around when you need them and then they interrupt
when you don't."

"Someone woke up on the wrong side of the bed this morning." Bill walked into the office and stopped in front of the desk.

"Ha. You'd be grouchy, too, if you were dealing with this."

Sara closed the file and stacked it neatly on the side of her desk. "This being my sister's latest legal entanglement."

Bill reached over and grabbed the file from the stack. A big grin broke out on his face.

"Renee told me Tasha called. What did I miss?"

"Only a cease and desist order from Dr. Heath Purdue, and a potential liability claim for slippery floors due to fuzzy pig slippers. Other than that, nothing."

Bill stared at Sara, then poked at his ear, as if trying to get water out.

"Can you run that by me again?" Bill sank into one of the overstuffed armchairs across from her. "I thought I heard something about pig slippers and the doctor who can get anyone pregnant, but that can't be right."

Sara considered her options: give Bill a play-by-play of Wednesday's events or let him read the file himself. She knew the play-by-play would take more time but create less confusion. Then she could hand off the case and get back to her other clients. She needed all the time she could get to draft the custody agreement determining who got Tiny, a 225-pound Saint Bernard, on weekends and holidays. She didn't understand why her client was so insistent he have Tiny for the summer solstice, but she would worry about that later.

Sara reviewed Tasha's predicament with Bill. He listened attentively and asked a few questions here and there before saying, "Do you think Doug is capable of the fake reviews?"

"I think he could have written the one that was from Tasha. It sounds like him. But the rest of them?" Sara shrugged. "He's not capable of that style of writing."

Bill reached out for the file and Sara handed it to him. After he flipped through it, he said, "Start there. Draft a letter to Purdue's attorney. Throw Doug under the bus. Remind the doctor that it was Doug, not Tasha, who made the initial stink when the children were born. Tell them they're going to need more than a review that could have been posted by anyone before they can issue a cease and desist against our client. Draft the letter. I'll review it."

"What do you mean, you'll review it? I thought I was getting you up to speed so you could handle it. She is your client, remember?" Sara didn't need another case. Her work with Tiny was complicated enough.

"And, she's your sister. You can handle this. It'll be good for you." Bill stood up and handed the file back to Sara. "Plus, this should be a good distraction from Tiny. I hear the summer solstice visitation is going to be tricky."

"Are you interested in hearing about the potential liability case for slippery floors?" Sara glared at her partner.

"Not really. I think the pigs can handle it." Bill grinned. "I heard Brad was here yesterday. Is there a problem with the hospital project?"

Sara frowned.

"He must have been in with Rich. I don't know what's going on. I didn't really talk to him with everything that happened."

"Doesn't matter. Glad Brad could help Tasha out. At least someone in that family has some manners. Don't forget to get me the draft." Bill tossed the file back on Sara's desk and walked out of her office.

Sara turned to her computer to draft a response, but after five minutes of staring at a blank screen, she pushed back from the desk and walked to her window. From there, she watched the people in the park, running around, throwing Frisbees to their dogs, enjoying the afternoon. Everyone seemed so happy.

She thought about what Bill said, about her being in a bad mood. Sara wished she could blame it on dealing with her sister. Usually, their interactions put her on edge, but Tasha seemed different this time around.

Maybe Mom is right. Sisters can be friends after they grow up.

But if she was honest, and Sara prided herself on honesty,

the real problem was her. She was disappointed Yoga Guy hadn't shown up for class on Wednesday night.

Sara was aware how pathetic pining over an imaginary boyfriend was, especially for someone her age. She didn't even know his real name or if he was in a relationship with someone else. The only conversation they ever had was when she asked if she could put her yoga mat next to his.

"Why sure. My pleasure," her Guy had said.

Sara had analyzed those words for days. Was it really a pleasure to have her next to him? Was he just being polite? She didn't know. She wondered if he was offended by her sweat, which was really stupid, considering it was a hot yoga class and everyone was sweating. Or maybe she just smelled worse than everyone else?

Now she was being ridiculous. It was silly to wonder if someone disliked her because she smelled when she worked out. Besides, there could be any number of reasons he didn't show up to class. He might have had to work late. Or maybe he is sick. Or dead.

"Get a hold of yourself, Sara." Her voice echoed in the empty office. "Stop procrastinating and focus."

She started back to her desk when the phone rang. She grabbed it on the second ring.

"Help! Tiny and his owner got here early. Mr. Robert is on the phone, fighting over the whole summer solstice custody thing. Can you get out here and take care of this please?" Renee begged; her voice urgent. "I don't want to clean up after that dog again, and he's getting nervous with the screaming."

Sara could hear her client's voice hurling insults. She hated it when two people who once loved one another reached the point when they couldn't stand each other. Splitting up assets was hard enough, but add a child, and it got a lot worse. She didn't think a dog custody agreement would be as contentious.

"I'll be right out." Sara hoped she could spare Renee clean-up duty.

As she pulled the receiver from her ear, Sara heard Mr. Robert's voice.

"Tiny, no, baby, no!"

Sara heard Renee's muttered curse. "Too late, Sara. You're too late."

19

Tasha walked into the hotel lobby. The sign-in table for the speed dating session stood outside the double doors of the meeting room. A heavily made-up woman in a strapless dress sat alone behind the table. Tasha thought the woman looked bored as she flipped through a magazine.

No one was waiting to check in, which surprised Tasha. She glanced at her watch. The session started in ten minutes.

Maybe no one will show up, and I can go home early. I could binge watch that hospital series.

It was crazy she let her mother talk her into this. She didn't like dating in general, so Tasha wasn't sure how she would like multiple dates in one evening. The bright spot was her "dates" were only ten minutes long, and she was under no obligation to see any of them again.

How bad could it be?

The woman didn't look up when Tasha approached. Since she wasn't paying attention, Tasha gave her a once-over. The woman's cleavage threatened to spill over the top of the red strapless dress. The dress was tight and fitted when the woman was sitting down. Tasha was scared to think what it would look like when she stood up. Strappy, sparkly high heels finished off the outfit. A recent blow out emphasized the woman's expertly highlighted blond hair. Tasha thought the woman looked like a model, ready to walk the runway.

Tasha realized her outfit of a blue silk shirt, black pants, and black ankle boots was better suited to a PTO meeting than a speed dating session. She had a bad feeling the rest of the women here would be dressed in something tight and flashy compared to her comfortable and conservative. Knowing there was nothing she could do about it now, Tasha cleared her throat to get the woman's attention. She might as well get the evening started.

The woman looked up and flashed a brilliant white smile at Tasha. The smile didn't make it all the way to the woman's eyes, which were framed in the longest fake lashes Tasha had ever seen. Tasha felt like she was being studied, which was only fair, as she had done the same thing.

"Can I help you?" The throaty sound of the woman's voice matched the sexy outfit she wore. "The Alcoholics Anonymous meeting is down the hall."

"No, I don't need AA, but thanks." The woman's comment should have offended Tasha, but it only confirmed she was underdressed for the evening. "I'm here for the speed dating session. I'm a few minutes early."

The woman unabashedly looked Tasha over from head to toe.

"Oh. Well. Then you're in the right place." Tasha thought the woman's tone of voice disagreed with her words. "You can sign in here. Go inside the banquet room and Tony will explain everything when it's time."

The woman returned to her magazine, leaving Tasha to follow the instructions. This wasn't the welcoming experience Tasha expected, but she filled out the sign-in sheet and went into the room. She understood what to do. She didn't think the eyelash queen would welcome any more questions.

The room itself wasn't particularly inviting, either. A man, probably Tony, stood at the front of the room by a table with a giant stopwatch. He read a magazine, too. Tasha smiled, but the man didn't look up. Not sure what else to do, Tasha wandered through the tables, looking for her name.

She was the only person in the room, other than Tony. It seemed odd no one else would be here, considering the session started in less than five minutes. She found her name on one of the tables. At least she was in the right place. Taking a seat, she put her name tag on and waited.

She sat for a few minutes until all of a sudden, a group of people rushed in the door. They scurried around the room, looking for their tables. Tasha looked toward Tony to explain the correct speed dating procedure, but what he said surprised her.

"All right, everyone. Take your seat. The time starts in three, two, one. Go."

Tasha realized she wasn't going to get an explanation of how the session worked at the same time she realized no one was sitting at her table. Several other people sat alone, empty seats across from them. She started to get up and move to another table, but Tony stopped her.

"Stay where you are. No switching tables until round two."

Tasha hoped her mother hadn't paid too much for this evening because it looked like it was going to be a bust. Tasha gazed around the room while she waited for the first round of "dating" to be finished. She realized all the empty seats should have held men. Four other women sat like she did, across from an empty chair.

Taking a mint from her purse, Tasha realized the odds were against her, even here. Not only were there more women than men, most of the women looked like the lady in the red dress at the sign-in desk. Tasha should have known fake boobs trumped a good personality any day of the week.

Tasha caught herself before she laughed out loud. The men tonight all seemed to be enjoying the artificial enhancements abounding in the room. She knew it was unfair to judge the men when it was clear this was not the kind of dating session meant to connect people in a long-term relationship. Booty call, yes. Marriage and children, no.

Not that she needed another marriage or more children. Look how well her first marriage went. Not only did Doug leave her for another woman, he also treated her like an ATM when he needed money.

I still don't understand how he can be broke. Maybe Sara can hire someone to find out. Or instead of speed dating, I could be trawling the Internet looking for whatever stupid thing Doug did to get him to come back here.

A high-pitched cackle brought Tasha back to the room. Glancing up, she saw a brunette flip her long wavy hair over her shoulder. Tasha did a double take when she noticed the woman's shirt. A skin-tight black tank top decorated with a sparkling wine glass outlined in rhinestones and the words "Screw It!" adorned the woman's torso.

"I am so out of place," Tasha mumbled to herself and wondered again why she'd agreed to this in the first place. Then she remembered. She hadn't agreed to this. Her mother tricked her into it. Helene used her grandchildren as leverage to get Tasha out of the house. As irritated as Tasha was, she gave her mom credit for using her resources wisely.

"Time's up. Date number two starts in one minute." Tony's voice carried through the room. "Women stay at your table. Men move to your left."

Tasha waited patiently for the man at the next table to sit down with her. She wasn't excited to meet him. He was wearing a muscle T-shirt and bedazzled jeans, and she could smell his cologne from where she was sitting. Wondering what she would say to him, Tasha's mouth dropped open in shock when he skipped her table and sat down at the next one, just as Tony signaled the start of the next session.

Frustration overwhelmed Tasha. She might not be dressed seductively, but that didn't give Bedazzled Boy the right to skip her. Tasha got up from her chair. She planned to tell him what she thought.

"You skipped a table, you know?" Tasha looked down at the man whose name was Jim, according to his name tag. "You were supposed to sit down at my table."

Jim appraised Tasha from head to toe.

"Yeah, why would I want to sit with you when I could sit with Honey here?" Jim nodded to the brunette across from him. Honey wore a tight leopard-print miniskirt with what could only be described as a barely-there matching tank top. Her eyes were painted with bright blue shadow and heavy black liner, and her shiny red lips matched the color of the apples Tasha packed in the kids' school lunches. Honey's black, lace-up, thigh-high boots finished off the ensemble.

Tasha shook her head and returned to her table. She could think of several reasons why she was a better choice than Honey, but Jim wasn't her type anyway. She should be glad he skipped her because she didn't think she could talk to a man wearing sparkles on his jeans for ten minutes.

Tony met her at her seat.

"Lady, you can't move. The men switch tables. The ladies sit," he said. "You'll get someone the next round."

"Is that a threat or a promise?" Frustration filled Tasha.

"Huh? Whadusay?" Tasha thought he sounded like the guys on one of the reality TV shows she watched.

"Nothing." She didn't want to irritate the man too much. The guys on the TV show were really rude, so she didn't know if Tony would be like them or not. "I am curious, though. Why do the guys get to pick whatever woman they want? That guy just skipped my table to go to Honey's. And there aren't even enough men for all the women here."

Tony smiled with teeth Tasha thought were too big and too white to be natural.

"It happens. Some nights are better for the guys, and sometimes the chicks have the advantage. You should come back another time and see."

"So, am I supposed to leave now?" Tasha frowned. "I haven't even had one conversation yet, unless you count this one."

"No, you can stay for the rest of the night. I gotta warn ya, though. The guys go for the hotties. You're more of the mom type."

"I am a mom. What's wrong with that?"

Tony put his hands up as if to calm her down.

"Don't get mad. This might not be your best crowd. We've got some older-age groups that might work better for you."

"Older. Thanks. That helps a lot."

"You're welcome." Tony walked back to his post, missing Tasha's sarcasm.

Tasha couldn't wait to call her mother and give her a piece of her mind. What was she thinking? Tasha wondered again how her mother found this group. Helene should know her own daughter well enough to realize she wouldn't fit in with this kind of crowd. If she ever did this again, she wanted to come to a "Normal, but having a bad couple of years" session.

And if there wasn't a category like that, she was going to request one.

20

"She has no idea, does she?" Carlton placed the knife and spoon to the right of the plate.

"Which she and what idea?" Brad stirred the pan on the stove, watching his partner move about the dining room. Brad enjoyed making dinner for Carlton. The couple's schedule was busy, but Brad knew how important it was to spend time together.

"You know what I'm talking about." Carlton placed the fork on top of the napkin. "Don't play dumb. And stop staring at me. I'm just setting the table."

"Actually, I don't know what you're talking about. There was no transition between the discussion about our next vacation and your question."

"Fair point. I'm referring to Tasha and the fact she has no idea we're together."

"See? Nothing to do with vacation." Brad tasted the food and threw in a pinch more salt. "And no. She doesn't."

"Why not? She needs to know, and she needs to find out from you. She has the right to know, especially since you're spending time with the kids. What if someone else tells her about us?" Carlton walked into the kitchen. "I'd be mad at you, and I'm nicer than Tasha."

Brad laughed.

"You're nicer than most people. I should tell Tasha, but I don't think it will matter to her. I haven't told Doug, either. Shouldn't I come out to my own brother first?"

"Why bother?" Carlton took two water glasses down from the cabinet. "Besides, he's never around, anyway."

"Actually, he's in town. Tasha ran into him at the mall."

The water glasses clinked as Carlton set them on the counter.

"The mall? I sent her to the mall!"

Before Carlton could get worked up, Brad interrupted, "Don't blame yourself. Doug would have tracked Tasha down, anyway. That's just the way he is." When Carlton began adding ice to the glasses, Brad said "Doug does whatever he wants without bothering to consider the consequences. It's all about him."

"If he's that bad, why did Tasha ever give him the time of day?" Carlton raised his hand in the air. "I know he's your brother, but the man sounds like an ass."

Brad shrugged.

"He used to be a pretty good guy. Before they won the lottery. All that money changed him, and not for the better. By the time it got really bad, Blake and Libby were here. I think Tasha wanted to keep the family intact. A dysfunctional family seemed better than a broken one."

Carlton shook his head as he carried the water glasses to the dining room. "Not a good reason as far as I'm concerned, but I didn't walk in her shoes. Back to the point: you need to tell her about us. She deserves to hear the facts from you."

"She does. I don't want her to think I'm like Doug. He lied to her for months about his girlfriend."

"So best not to lie to her about your boyfriend, don't you

think?" Carlton stared at Brad.

"I hate it when you're right. She deserves better. So do Libby and Blake. They're great kids. It's too bad they got stuck with a crappy father. It's stupid that Doug doesn't spend any time with them. China doesn't care for them for some reason."

"You know what I think about her—"

"Yes, you've made yourself perfectly clear, Carlton. China is a home-wrecking whore who shouldn't have a real estate license." Brad chuckled. "Although you never explained why she shouldn't be able to sell houses."

"Any person who destroys a family home should not be licensed to sell a house."

Brad watched as Carlton carried the food from the kitchen into the dining room, amazed at how Carlton connected things. China could sell a house, but Carlton questioned if she had what it took to create a home. Brad would let his brother worry about that.

"Carlton, you have a way with words. And I love you for it. You're right. I should tell Tasha before she finds out herself although I don't know who'd tell her."

"Not me, that's for sure. She was a mess the other day in the office. And those pig slippers!"

"I told you, she was having a bad day on Wednesday." Brad sat down at the table. "She went to see her sister about some loose ends, and that's when she fell in the lobby."

Carlton sat across from Brad.

"Her sister is an attorney, correct?"

Brad nodded as he began dishing out the pork chops and scalloped potatoes.

"Isn't that a conflict of interest?" asked Carlton. "Using a relative as your attorney?"

"She told me Bill and Rich were in meetings, so Sara was helping her out. I'm sure it's fine. Sara's a great attorney. She's done some work for me on occasion when Rich was busy."

"Why were you there, anyway? Is something going on with work?" Carlton let out a low whistle. "These pork chops are fantastic. What did you do to them?"

"It's all in the seasoning. I found the recipe somewhere online." Brad returned to the original conversation. "The business is fine. I meet with Rich once a year to review contracts and documents. Most of it's standard, but I like having a second set of eyes on things every now and then. Don't you have an attorney who reviews your business?"

"No. Once I set everything up, I just assumed it was fine the way it was. Ongoing legal counsel sounds expensive, and I didn't see the need."

"It's cheaper than going to court, which is why I do it. Plus, things change. You need to keep up with new business laws." Brad pointed at Carlton with his fork. "Why don't you make an appointment with Sara? She's good. She could review everything and tell you if anything needs updating."

"Why can't I use Rich?"

"Not a good fit. I can't see you and Rich working well together. Sara's more your style. She's professional but can carry a conversation. I think Rich would bore you to tears."

"Isn't that what a lawyer is supposed to do?"

"You know what I mean. Give the office a call and set something up with Sara. You might not need to do anything, but she'll be a good resource for you."

"Does she wear pig slippers to work?" Carlton asked.

"No pig slippers. Manolos or Louboutins are more her style. You'll be fine with her. She's great. She's completely different from her sister."

"If you say so. I'll call on Monday." Carlton wiped his mouth and pushed back his chair. "I need to get this all cleaned up. I want to go to a hot yoga tonight.

"You go. I'll clean up. I need to finish some work so I can go to Blake's soccer game tomorrow." Brad folded his napkin. "Hey, do you want to join me? Depending on how things go, we could talk to Tasha about us. Maybe if she got used to us as friends, she'll be okay with us as partners."

"We can't tell her at the soccer game. Definitely not the right time." Carlton stood up and took his plate to the kitchen. "But Tasha mentioned Blake's game to me. I could say I was in the neighborhood and wanted to see how she was doing. I would like to meet Libby and Blake. Tasha adores them, and you clearly love them, too."

"Good. It's a date." Brad followed Carlton into the kitchen. "You and me at a seven-year-old's soccer game."

"I have suggestions for better date locations, but I'm late. I've got to change if I'm going to yoga."

"What yoga shorts are you wearing?"

"Probably the ugly gray ones." Brad noticed a worried expression on Carlton's face. "There's this woman who's been staring at me for weeks. I'm trying everything to turn her off. I think she wants to ask me out."

"Tell her you're dating someone."

"She seems so intense. She must have a stressful job. It takes her half the session to relax." He paused for a second, like he was deciding if he should say anything else. "And I swear I heard her call me Yoga Guy one day under her breath. Isn't that weird?"

"I think you're imagining things. But if you stand here thinking about her any longer, you're never going to make it to class."

Carlton gave Brad a quick peck on the cheek. "Fine. I'm gone. I'll see you later."

Brad couldn't resist. "Hey, Carlton? You should wear the neon-green shorts. You'll definitely stand out. Your lady friend will enjoy herself tonight."

Carlton gave his partner the finger, blew him a kiss, and left. Satisfied with the reaction, Brad got to work on the dishes.

21

"Defense, Blake! Get back on defense!" Tasha sighed. Blake was out of position again. He was past the midfield line, too far upfield for a defender. Blake knew he should stay close to his team's goal, but when he got excited, he forgot. Tasha imagined how exhilarated her son was now that his team were up by five goals.

"You're going to lose your voice if you keep yelling," Brad said. "I don't know any ear, nose, and throat docs who work weekends."

"Funny. I'm not going to lose my voice." Tasha kept her eyes on Blake. "He needs to get back in position."

"The coach will tell him. Relax and enjoy the game."

Tasha glanced at Brad. It was good having him there. Blake was thrilled he'd followed through on his promise and Libby enjoyed the strawberry and banana smoothie he'd brought her. And the hazelnut latte he'd given her was fantastic. Tasha started to say thank you but was interrupted as the crowd cheered. Blake's team scored again.

"This might be another mercy rule game." Tasha sipped her coffee.

"Another? I didn't know Blake's team was this good."

"For seven-year-olds, they are. They still bunch up around the ball, but most of the boys can kick with some degree of accuracy. It helps when the coach works with them as much as Greg does."

"Greg? Is that Greg White, Doug's friend from high school?" Brad looked across the field. "I didn't realize he was the team coach."

"He took over a couple of months ago. The last coach, Paul —I don't think you knew him—quit when he and his wife had another baby. His older son still plays, but he doesn't have time to coach. Greg is single and works from home, so Paul talked him into it. Paul told him he'd meet all kinds of women this way."

"Did Paul also tell him the women were married with children?"

Tasha laughed. "He left that part out. Greg seems to enjoy it though. I thought Doug might come to more of the games once Greg was the coach, but that didn't pan out, either. Sons and old friends don't rank as high as China."

Tasha pretended to focus on the game, but she was distracted. She kept looking around the park, half expecting Doug to show up. He hadn't contacted her since their run-in at the mall on Wednesday. For all she knew, he went back to St. Thomas with his girlfriend.

She hated knowing her ex-husband put everything before his children. She knew complaining wouldn't change it. It also wasn't fair to complain to Brad about his brother.

Enjoy the present. The kids are happy that Uncle Brad came through on his promise to watch the soccer game.

The sight of her parents walking from the parking lot surprised Tasha. They hadn't mentioned they were coming to the game when she picked the kids up that morning. She called to them and waved.

"Were you expecting your parents today?" said Brad.

"No, they came to last week's game. I wonder why they decided to come to this one too? They didn't say anything to me about it."

Helene and Max, Tasha's dad, stopped to give Libby a hug. Tasha watched them as they talked to their granddaughter. Max laughed at something Libby said when Tasha noticed someone else walking in from the parking lot. Tasha thought he looked familiar. At first, she was afraid it was Doug. Then she realized it was Carlton, the chiropractor who fixed her shoulder. She glanced back at Brad, who waved at Carlton.

"Is that your chiropractor? What's he doing here?"

"Yeah. That's Carlton."

"That's odd. I've never seen him at a game before. Maybe he knows someone who plays for the other team?"

Brad coughed and cleared his throat.

"Yeah, I don't know." Tasha thought he sounded funny when he continued, "I'll just go and say hi."

"Okay." Tasha's focus returned to the game. "Fall back, Blake! You're on defense."

Blake rushed back to the goal area to help his teammates. One of the players kicked the ball out of bounds. Despite Coach Greg's repeated request to stay on the field, the game came to a standstill as several players chased after it.

Chuckling at the situation, Tasha turned to watch Brad. He stood next to Carlton, pointing toward her. Tasha waved and Carlton waved back. The men started to walk toward her but stopped when Helene called out to Brad. She couldn't hear exactly what her mother said, but the two men detoured to where her parents were standing.

Tasha shook her head. Knowing her mother, Helene would finagle an appointment with Carlton in the next five minutes. She watched as Brad introduced Carlton to them then waited. Her mother always engaged in pleasantries, but it never failed. Helene had no problem asking for what she wanted.

Too bad Tasha didn't inherit that trait.

As the soccer ball rolled back on the field, Tasha saw Brad and Carlton walk to the parking lot as her parents headed her way. It surprised her that Brad didn't bring Carlton over to say hello, but it wasn't any of her business. The men might have something important to discuss.

Helene and Max joined Tasha on the sidelines.

"Another mercy rule game?" Max looked at the scoreboard. "What is it? Five goals ahead of the other team?"

"Six. It kinda looks like the game will be over soon. The boys are playing well together."

"Libby doesn't seem interested in the game, now does she?" Helene looked back at Libby. Tasha saw her daughter doing somersaults, ignoring the soccer game completely.

"She usually isn't. As long as she has someone to hang with, she's good. Why are you guys here? I wasn't expecting you."

"Blake left his backpack at the house when you picked him up. We thought he might need it for school tomorrow." Max put the backpack on the ground. "Plus, we were supposed to meet Sara here."

Tasha's eyes widened. "Sara's coming? Really? She usually works on Sundays. How'd she get the schedule?"

"I gave it to her. I thought it would be nice for her to see the kids." Helene clapped as her grandson's team scored again. "She canceled on us though. Said she needed to work. She needs to get out more often."

"You could always sign her up for speed dating," said Tasha. The image of her sister in a navy-blue business suit with pearls standing next to Honey in her miniskirt and thigh-high boots made her smile. "It might be right up her alley."

Helene turned and stared at her younger daughter.

"That's not a bad idea," said Helene, tapping her chin as the idea percolated. "I wonder if they have another session Sara could attend. I don't want you two fighting over men."

Tasha and her dad laughed at the same time.

"I'm pretty sure there won't be any fighting," said Tasha as she thought about the men she met the night before. "Sara is welcome to any one of those guys who were there last night."

"Make sure I'm not around when you float this idea to Sara," said Max, putting his arms around his wife and daughter. "Sweetheart, I love you for wanting to help our children, but this speed dating thing is pushing the limits, even for you."

"If I didn't push, no one would." Helene gave her husband a peck on the cheek before looking over to where Brad and Carlton stood. "It's not like with the two of them. They figured it out on their own."

Tasha saw her dad tense up at the same time as her mother's face flushed.

"What are you talking about now, Mom?"

"Helene. Stay out of it," warned Max.

"Out of what, Dad?"

Before Max could respond, shouting filled the air. Someone was on the field screaming at one of the players. She couldn't tell who it was at first. A man stood in the middle of a group of defenders, making a racket. She wondered what Blake thought about the delay of the game.

Then, it hit her. She knew that voice. Her back stiffened and her stomach rolled. Max and Helene seemed to understand what was going on after it registered with Tasha.

"Do you want help or do you want to talk to him yourself?"

"Thanks, Dad, but I don't think there will be any talking." Tasha sprinted onto the soccer field toward her ex-husband.

22

"**D**efenders never pass midline, Blake. How stupid are you?" Doug stood in front of his son, his face flushed. The rest of the team huddled behind Blake. They seemed scared to get close to Doug but didn't want to leave Blake alone. By the time she made it to the scene, Tasha saw that the coach and several other parents had joined the group.

"Hey, Doug, it's okay. They're learning. Blake's doing a great job," Greg assured him. "I know you haven't seen him in a while, but he's good, man."

Tasha stopped in front of Blake. For a minute, the soccer field was quiet. Then she heard people mumbling around her.

"What was she thinking, marrying that creep?"

"Who would do that to a little boy?"

"He always was a jerk."

Tasha caught her breath before she spoke.

"Why are you still here in town?"

"I don't have to tell you everything." Doug spat onto the ground. "Why do you let him play like this? He should know better by now. He's playing like a girl."

"This isn't the time or the place, Doug. Walk off the field and let them finish the game." Tasha remained in front of her son. "Greg's on top of it. He's the coach. He'll handle it."

"So, it's okay for you to yell at him and not me, that's what you're saying?"

"How long have you been here?"

Doug looked over to where Brad and Carlton were standing. "Long enough."

The referee came over and blew his whistle.

"All parents off the field so we can continue the game." The referee walked over to Greg and said something under his breath. Greg frowned, but he nodded and turned to Tasha and Doug.

"Doug, if you don't leave, the kids forfeit the game. Can you go to the parking lot and finish this later? It isn't fair to the kids. They're winning right now."

Doug glared at Greg.

"You're on her side now?"

Greg threw his hands in the air.

"I'm not on anyone's side. I'm just coaching the game. Let them finish the game, and then you can have your say." No one else spoke, but several dads stepped up behind Greg in silent support.

Doug cursed under his breath and then turned.

"I'll be in the parking lot, Tasha. Don't think this is over."

Greg called the kids back together as the rest of the parents left the field. Tasha put her hand on Blake's shoulder.

"You okay?"

His eyes were full of unshed tears. He nodded, but she could see how upset he was.

"You're doing great, Blake. You are. Don't let anyone tell you otherwise."

"I was too far past the line." A tear finally rolled down Blake's cheek. "But I'm not stupid. And I don't play like a girl."

"No, you're not stupid. And girls can be good soccer players, too." Blake gave his mom a little smile. "It's okay to be upset. I understand if you don't want to finish the game. But your team needs you. I think you should shake it off and get back out there. Show him you know how to play."

Tasha saw the spark of competitiveness return to Blake's eyes.

"Okay." He started back toward his team, then Blake ran back to Tasha. He gave her a big hug. "I love you, Mom. I'll do good!"

Blake returned to his team, and Tasha headed back to where her parents stood on the sidelines. On her way over, she saw a bright red sports car in the parking lot. Doug sat in the driver's seat. He didn't turn the engine on. He sat there and stared.

Struggling to keep a look of composure on her face, guilt washed over her. While she wanted Doug to pay attention to his children, this wasn't what she meant. Tasha guessed Doug's presence at the game had more to do with his business proposal than anything. She should have told him no at the mall. He was like a predator circling its prey. He smelled her indecision and planned to take advantage of it.

The referee blew his whistle and the game restarted as Tasha stepped between her mom and dad. She felt their arms embrace her, and she released a little bit of the tension she carried.

This is exactly what I need. Parental support.

"I thought I'd seen everything. I wouldn't have believed that outburst if I hadn't seen it for myself." Helene squeezed Tasha's arm. "I'm so glad we don't have to put up with him anymore. I never understood what you saw in him, anyway."

Check that: nonjudgmental support.

"Helene, now is not the time. Tasha didn't do anything wrong." The words *this time* sounded in her head even though her father didn't say them. Max continued. "What are you going to do about this, Natasha? You can't let him treat you like this. What's your plan?"

Tasha's shoulders slumped. She hated confrontation, but if she didn't stand up to Doug now, it was only going to get worse. But what could she do?

"Max is right. Why don't you let Carlton and I take the kids to get pizza after the game?" Brad's eyes conveyed sympathy, which made Tasha glad for his presence and ashamed he witnessed his brother's actions. "Let your parents help you. I don't think you should talk to him alone."

"No, I shouldn't, but he won't like it if you take the kids. He doesn't want you around them, remember? And why is Carlton here, anyway?"

"Doug can't tell me what to do." Brad shrugged.

"You invited me to Blake's game on Wednesday. Don't you remember?" Tasha saw Carlton glance at Brad. "You were so excited about the game, I thought I'd just stop by."

"Oh yeah. Probably not the best game to witness, but thanks for coming." Tasha didn't remember inviting Carlton, but Wednesday wasn't her finest hour. She pressed her fingers to her temples. "Okay. I need to talk to Doug."

Max tightened his grip on his daughter. "You shouldn't talk with Doug alone. It probably shouldn't be here either. Helene, call Sara and tell her what happened. Maybe she or Bill or Rich can set up a meeting for tomorrow. Someone official needs to be with Tasha when she talks with him."

Helene nodded and pulled her cell phone from her purse. "I'll check on Libby, too," she said and walked toward her granddaughter.

As Helene walked away, Tasha recalled her mother's comment from earlier.

"Dad, what did you stop Mom from saying before Doug showed up?" Tasha struggled out of her father's embrace. "You told her to stay out of it. Did you know Doug was going to be here today? Why would you keep that from me? I need to know this stuff."

Max looked at Brad, who glanced at Carlton. Carlton shrugged and smiled at Tasha.

"I know I'm the outsider here, but maybe you all should focus on the game and talk about this afterward."

Both Max and Brad nodded.

"He's right. Here's what you're going to do. I will walk over to Doug and tell him someone will call him tomorrow with a time to meet. Brad and Carlton can load the kids up after the game." Max stared intently at Brad. The expression on her father's face reminded her of when Blake and Libby tried to send telepathic messages to each other: his forehead crinkled, and his nose scrunched up. "We can all drive to the pizza place. I'll call in an order so if we need to, we can just take the pizza home. Don't let Doug spoil anything else, Tasha. Let us help you."

Something felt off to Tasha, but she didn't have the time or energy to figure out what it was. Pushing aside the feeling, she said, "Fine. But as soon as the kids are in bed, I want some answers."

23

Tasha slumped against the wall. Doug's behavior at the game exhausted her. The lively victory dinner at the pizza place didn't help either. Blake and Libby's longer-than-normal bedtime routine zapped what little energy Tasha had left. If it weren't for the fact that her parents, Brad, and Carlton were waiting for her in the living room, she would have headed straight to bed. Unfortunately, sleep would have to wait.

Pushing off the wall, she shuffled to the living room, the oinking of her pig slippers announced her arrival.

"I don't know why you keep those." Helene shook her head. "I'll think twice the next time the kids want to get you a gift."

Brad stood by the window, a glass of wine in each hand. He lifted one of the glasses.

"I thought you might want a drink after today," said Brad.

"It's a school night, but what the heck." She took the glass, staring at its contents. "I did want to say thank you for helping today. I'm glad I have you guys for support." Tasha looked around the room, and asked, "Where's Carlton? I hope Doug didn't scare him off."

"No, it takes more than that to spook him. He has an early appointment tomorrow." Brad took a sip of wine. "He also thought you'd be more comfortable if he wasn't here."

The suspicious feeling from the soccer game returned. Tasha noticed Max and Helene exchanged a look and Brad studied the floor. They all looked guilty to her, but she didn't know why. Frustrated, Tasha stamped her foot to the ground. Her slipper gave a high-pitched squeak. Three pairs of eyes focused on her.

Blushing at her juvenile behavior, Tasha said, "Now that I have your attention, can someone please tell me what's going on? Did you all know Doug was going to be at the game?"

Shaking his head, Max said, "No. Doug was an unpleasant surprise for us all." He nodded at Brad. "You better tell her now. Whatever she's imagining is worse than the truth."

As her stomach tied itself in knots, Tasha turned toward Brad.

"Tell me what?" said Tasha.

"This isn't the best timing with Doug's little performance today, but before you find out from someone else, I wanted to tell you. Carlton is not just my chiropractor." Brad paused, looking at Max and Helene before returning his gaze to her. "He is my life partner. We live together."

Tasha didn't know what to say. She didn't care one way or the other, but she expected to talk about Doug tonight. Not Brad's boyfriend.

Whoa. Brad has a boyfriend?

Before she could speak, Helene jumped in.

"Life partner? I thought you said he was your boyfriend. What does a life partner have to do with being gay? Why do you need a life partner? You already know what to do with your life. You're an architect. Dr. Reynolds is a chiropractor, not a life partner. Did I miss something?"

Before she could stop it, a giggle slipped from Tasha's

mouth. She covered her mouth with her hand, but it didn't help. The giggle was infectious because Max and Brad joined in. Her mother, however, did not.

"Why are you laughing at me?" Helene crossed her arms over her chest. "Are you making fun of me?"

Tasha tried to stop laughing, but she couldn't. She glanced at Brad for help.

"Helene, you've misunderstood. Carlton is my boyfriend. Sometimes, I refer to him as my life partner. A life coach is someone who helps you decide what to do with your life. I'm sorry if I confused you."

"Oh, thank heavens. Now I understand. Thank you, Brad, for explaining." Helene turned back to her daughter with a scowl. "It was a simple mistake. I don't know why you're laughing."

"Before my lovely bride gets anything else confused tonight, I'll take her home. Brad, take care of my daughter, please. She's had a long day. We'll let ourselves out."

Helene dawdled, but Max hustled her out, for which Tasha was grateful. She needed to talk to Brad without her mother's interruptions. As the front door closed, Tasha put down her glass of wine and walked to Brad. Without a word, she gave him a bear hug. This announcement made sense, and Tasha wanted to show Brad she didn't care one way or another who he lived with.

"I'm sorry I laughed, but I've had a long day. Doug's show wore me out."

"I get it. He wears us all out," said Brad. He pulled back from their embrace and looked Tasha in the eyes. "I want you to know this is not the way I planned to tell you about Carlton and me. I'm sorry about that. But I'm not sorry about who I am."

"No, you shouldn't be. I'm not... I'm just..." Tasha shrugged. "I don't know what to say."

"You don't have to say anything. I'm glad you finally know."

"Why didn't you tell me before? Hell, why couldn't I have figured it out on my own?" Tasha ran her hand through her hair. "I thought I knew you pretty well. Doug doesn't know, does he? Wow. I'm rambling. I probably don't even make sense."

"You've had a lot to handle today. Don't worry about it. But to answer your question about Doug, no. He doesn't know. You know as well as I do, my brother would not accept it. Look what he did to Blake today, and that was over a soccer game. He'd explode if he knew."

Tasha met Brad's smile with her own.

"I'm happy for you. You've found someone. That's great." Tasha couldn't help adding, "Although I'm surprised you told my mother before me."

"I didn't tell her. She figured it out."

"How did that happen?" asked Tasha.

"I'm still not entirely sure. Helene asked me if Carlton was my boyfriend when I saw her at the game today. And then your dad said they always knew. I didn't want to lie. It's kind of nice to be honest with people."

"My mother is like that. She doesn't mean any harm. She's just nosy." Tasha picked up her wine glass and took a sip. "But my dad. I didn't see that one coming."

"Neither did I." Brad looked out the window again. "I'm not sure my parents would have taken the news as well as they did."

She knew how conservative Doug and Brad's parents were. Tasha had addressed them as Mr. and Mrs. Gerome throughout her marriage. They blamed her for the divorce, even though it was Doug who cheated and left her and the kids.

"They don't know?"

"I haven't told them, but they won't be happy to hear the news. I can hear my father. He'll say something about how I'll tarnish the Gerome family name."

"Hmm. I wonder what your dad would think of Doug's performance today. If being gay is tarnishing, what does it mean when you're a jerk?"

Her comment earned her a smile.

"Tell me about Carlton. How did you meet him?" said Tasha.

"We were at a Chamber of Commerce meeting. It was a networking event. No one wanted to talk to him." Brad held up his hand. "Not because he's gay. Because he's a chiropractor."

"Yes, I can see that. Chiropractors have a bad reputation," joked Tasha.

Brad smiled as he continued.

"We talked. We have similar interests. I gave him some contacts for marketing. He introduced me to some clients. I got the hospital renovation job because of him."

"That worked well. Did Carlton get as good of a deal as you?"

"Well, he got me, so that's something." Brad laughed.

"You look good together. He's a nice guy. A great chiropractor, that fact I know first-hand."

"You really are okay with this, aren't you?" Brad sounded serious.

"Why wouldn't I be?"

"Some people don't understand."

"Understand what? That people are different? That people like who they like. You can't control who you are." She wanted to make Brad laugh again. "And even if I didn't agree, I'm not in the position to judge anyone. I'm a single mom whose ex-husband just screamed at her son in public, remember?"

"I'm being serious, Tasha."

"So am I, Brad. I'm fine. You're fine. Carlton's fine. We're all fine."

"Good. I wasn't sure what I was going to do if it bothered you."

"Who cares if it bothers me?" said Tasha. "This is your life, and you need to do what you need to do."

"Have you ever considered taking your own advice?"

Tasha's wine glass stopped en route to her mouth as the question hit her. Was she so concerned with what everyone else wanted from her that she hadn't considered what she needed? Ever since the divorce, she put the kids first and herself second. No, that wasn't true either. She still put Doug before herself. Even after all the horrible things Doug did, she kept the window of communication open. She hoped Doug would step up to the plate and be the person she wanted him to be.

Brad was right. This was her life. The only person she was hurting by holding on was herself. When she hurt herself, she couldn't be the mom she wanted to be for Blake and Libby. She couldn't be the woman she deserved to be. Holding on gave Doug more power.

As she processed her epiphany, Tasha took a big gulp of wine.

"I take it from your silence and wine consumption that I have offended you."

Brad's statement broke her contemplation and caused her to choke on her wine.

After Brad thumped her a few times on the back, Tasha caught her breath.

"Sorry about that. Wine went down the wrong pipe. No, you didn't offend me. I was thinking you were on to something. I've made a lot of mistakes in life. Marrying Doug was one of them."

"Stop beating yourself up, Tasha."

"Let me finish. When I fell the other day in Sara's office, I keep telling myself how stupid I was. I know better than leaving the house with my slippers on." Tasha raised her hand to stop Brad from interrupting. "But I have to say, falling in Sara's office turned out to be my best mistake."

Brad frowned.

"How so?"

Tasha walked to the couch and sat down.

"If I hadn't fallen, I wouldn't have ever figured out how much Sara worries about me. Carlton wouldn't have worked his magic on my neck, and I wouldn't be sitting in my living room sharing a glass of wine with you. As far as mistakes go that one was the best." She waved to Brad with her glass. "Come sit down."

She let him join her on the couch before she continued.

"Pardon me if I sound like a self-help book, but I had to make the mistakes to get where I need to be. Why not embrace the mistake and hold onto the good part?" She took a sip of wine. "The bad part is still here though. I have to deal with Doug."

"Helene said you have some other issue to address as well."

Puzzled by Brad's comment, Tasha asked, "What are you talking about?"

"Dr. Purdue. Your mom told me he sent you a letter. Something about submitting bad reviews and maligning his character."

Tasha closed her eyes and rubbed her temple with her free hand. She'd completely forgotten about the endocrinologist with all the other events of the day. Another wave of weariness came over her as she considered that predicament.

"She wasn't supposed to tell anyone about that."

"Did you really think your mother could keep a secret?"

Peeking out of one eye, Tasha said, "No. She can't. As much as she tries, it's impossible."

"What are you going to do about it?"

"Sara's working on it. I'll do what she tells me to do, I guess." Tasha put her glass down on the end table and cradled her head in her hands. "Do you think it's my fault Doug showed up today?"

Brad snorted, and she felt his hand on her shoulder.

"Please. When has *no* ever stopped Doug?"

They sat in companionable silence for a few minutes when Brad nudged her.

"Why don't I get out of here so you can get some rest? You've got a lot going on this week, and I can tell you're exhausted."

"Good idea." She took his wine glass and set it next to hers. "Let me walk you out."

With her pig slippers quietly oinking, Tasha led the way to the front door. As she held the door open, Brad turned to her and said, "Thank you, Tasha."

"For what?"

"For being you. For accepting me and Carlton. For not letting what my brother did today impact our friendship."

Tasha leaned in to give him another hug and hide the tears that welled up at his words.

"Thank you," said Tasha. She knew her voice betrayed the tears in her eyes, but she couldn't help it. "You kept me sane and showed me how lucky I am to have family like you in my life."

They said good night, and Tasha closed the door behind him. She leaned against the door as the emotions of the day washed over her. While she calmed down, she listened to the sounds of Brad leaving. His footsteps as he walked to his truck. The cab door opened and closed. The engine coming to life. The clunk of the transmission as it shifted into reverse. And finally, the sound of the truck fading as it got further and further down the street.

Tasha started toward her bedroom when the empty wine glasses caught her attention. About to leave them until the morning, she thought about her new housecleaner and picked up the glasses, along with a stack of magazines and a water glass. In the kitchen, she threw the magazines in the recycle can and put the glasses in the dishwasher. She loaded the breakfast bowls from the sink as well, added detergent, and started the machine.

With the promise of clean dishes in the morning, Tasha headed to bed.

24

D oug watched Brad's truck pull away from Tasha's house.

"About time."

He grabbed the bottle of whiskey from the passenger's seat and took a swig. The liquid burned going down but it numbed his anger. The day hadn't turned out the way he planned.

When he hatched the scheme to attend Blake's soccer game, he planned to act like the supportive father. Doug figured if he cheered on Blake and said something nice to the girl, Tasha would come around and give him the money he needed. She was like a dog. Give her a little attention and she followed you around forever. If things had gone like he wanted, he'd be on a plane to St. Thomas right now.

He never expected to find his brother at the soccer game, nor had he anticipated his own reaction. He felt his blood pressure rise just thinking about it. Brad had no right being there. It was all his brother's fault Doug lost his temper with Blake.

On top of that, his father-in-law thought he could have a heart-to-heart talk with him at the game.

"Doug, you're going to regret how you talked to Blake today.

I don't know what's gotten into you, but Tasha isn't your wife anymore. You can't tell her, or the kids what to do. If you want something, you need to work through the attorneys. I know you have the number."

"What gives him the right to tell me what to do?" Doug asked the empty car. If the old man thought he could stop Doug from getting what he wanted from Tasha, he had another thing coming. "Think again, Max."

He came out of his reverie as he saw Tasha's silhouette pass the living room window. Doug squinted to get a better look at what she was doing. She picked something up before walking toward the kitchen. Doug shook his head when he realized she was tidying up the living room.

Hell has frozen over. The woman is cleaning.

The lights went off in the living room, and his curiosity got the better of him. He looked around to see if anyone would notice him. The red rental car seemed like a good idea a few days ago, but Doug regretted his decision. The extra hit to his struggling finances was bad enough, but the sports car made it hard to be incognito. He should have taken the nondescript four-door sedan the rental company originally offered.

"Who knew I was going to play spy?"

He chugged some more whiskey, then got out of the car. The street was quiet enough. No neighborhood watch volunteers out tonight. He jogged across the street, making as little noise as possible. When he reached the house, Doug stepped over the squeaky middle step and crept onto the front porch. He positioned himself below the window and peeked in.

Tasha stood at the sink, loading the dishwasher. He didn't know what to think. Maybe he'd had too much whiskey, but was his wife now a neat freak? He did his best to assess the condition on the living room. The usual pile of laundry wasn't lying next to the chair. The kids' toys were nowhere in sight.

Even the stack of magazines Tasha kept by the couch was gone. She must have turned over a new leaf.

Doug heard a car turn onto the street and pressed himself into the shadows. He didn't want to be caught spying on his wife. Doug held his breath until the car pulled up to a house down the block. Exhaling, he looked through the window in time to see Tasha flick the light switch off and head to her bedroom. Figuring there was nothing he could do right now, Doug ran across the street and got back into the car.

As he slid onto the leather seat, he said, "Think. What do I do now?"

Grabbing the whiskey, he took another gulp before shoving the lid back on the bottle and stuffing it under the passenger's seat. He couldn't afford to get pulled over on the drive to the hotel.

The best thing to do right now was to drive back to the hotel and sleep off his buzz. By tomorrow morning, the anger and resentment from the day should be gone. He'd be able to talk some sense into Tasha. If he had to, he would call Sara and set up a meeting. He hated wasting the time and money, but he knew sometimes you had to spend money to make money. This trip was about making money.

Easing the car away from the curb, Doug drove down the block before turning on his lights. The last thing he needed was for Tasha to suspect he was watching her. Then he'd never get what he wanted.

25

Tasha breathed a sigh of relief. The two-hour PTO meeting was over. She was free at last. She needed to write herself a sticky note.

"Never go to a PTO meeting again!"

While it was good to be up to speed with the school gossip, there had to be a better way. Trading precious hours of her life that she will never get back to find out that Oliver and Olivia's father was actually a client of her sister's wasn't the best use of her time. Especially when she could have asked Sara. Although knowing her, Sara would have stuck with client confidentiality and not told her a thing.

She forgot how tedious the meetings were. Who cared if the students sold wrapping paper or cookie dough for a fundraiser? Nobody wanted either. To make things worse, she agreed to be on the Welcoming Committee. The upside was she would get to talk to some new parents. The downside was she was obligated to attend meetings for the rest of the school year.

She'd worry about that later. There was enough time before the kids got out of school to run some errands. Tasha was halfway out the door when she heard her name.

"Ms. Gerome, do you have a few moments?" said Ms. May. "I want to share something with you. It's about Blake."

Tasha's stomach plummeted. Being called to the principal's office made her feel like a kid again, even if she hadn't done anything wrong. In this case, one of her children had, so it was guilt by association.

Pasting a smile on her face, Tasha nodded her acceptance and followed Ms. May into her office.

"Please take a seat," said Ms. May. "I'm glad I caught you."

"Is there a problem?"

"I want you to look at something." Ms. May sat behind her desk and shuffled some papers. She found what she wanted and placed it in front of Tasha. "Blake drew this picture for Mrs. Anderson. She requested students draw something their family did this past weekend."

Tasha glanced at the picture of a mom and dad smiling behind a son and daughter. Tasha felt a stab of sadness. Blake's family pictures usually consisted of three people: Tasha, Libby, and himself. Sunday's run-in with Doug must have confused him more than she thought. He included Doug in his family again. Swallowing hard, Tasha decided the best way to handle the principal was head on.

"I'm not sure I understand," said Tasha. "Is he not allowed to include his father?"

"I didn't see it at first, either, but Mrs. Anderson brought it to my attention. Take a closer look."

She studied the picture. Blake drew his family of four, holding hands under a tree. Everyone was smiling big goofy grins. Blake drew lots of details. Tasha wore her favorite sundress with flowers. Libby's hair was in pigtails with her favored pink bows. Blake donned his soccer jersey and shin guards, and Doug's striped shirt matched the one Brad wore to Sunday's game.

Tasha wondered why Doug would be wearing Brad's

clothes when she noticed the bright red car in the background. Squinting at the car, Tasha saw a tiny head looking out the window toward the family. The face was frowning.

Then she saw the names.

Under each person, Blake wrote their name. Hers, Libby's, and Blake's names were where she expected them, but Brad and Doug's were not. Brad turned out to be the man smiling with the soccer ball tucked under his arm. Doug sat in the car, glaring at the rest of the family.

Tasha didn't know what to say. She knew Blake liked having his uncle around, but she underestimated how much. She was glad she didn't have to show this to Doug though. He would never understand why Blake drew the picture. Ms. May interrupted Tasha's thoughts.

"I know you and Mr. Gerome divorced. Mrs. Anderson and I are aware of your family issues. But do you think this is the way to solve your problems?"

"What?" Tasha looked away from the picture. "How does this picture solve my problems?"

"Ms. Gerome, you've been through a lot. Libby and Blake have, too. I am impressed by how you have handled your ex-husband's eccentricities, but I have to be honest with you. Taking up with your ex-husband's brother is wrong."

Tasha cleared her throat to cover the laugh that threatened. Ms. May thought she was dating Brad? If only the principal knew how absurd the accusation was.

"I'm not. Not seeing Brad, that is. I guess I see how you might come to that conclusion but trust me, Brad is not the least bit interested in me."

Ms. May looked skeptical.

"But you're interested in him?"

Tasha sighed. She wasn't about to tell the principal about Brad and Carlton. She did need to pull herself together and set Ms. May straight.

"No, I'm not interested in Brad. I'm actually dating. Someone else." Tasha neglected to clarify that she was speed dating, but Ms. May didn't need to know that. "Brad stepped in to help me with the kids. That's all. Doug came back this weekend and wasn't happy. Why are you so concerned about this, anyway? Is Blake in trouble? He didn't do anything, did he?"

"You don't think this is a cry for help? Mrs. Anderson feels Blake is confused."

"I appreciate the concern, but we're fine." Tasha changed the subject. "How is Libby doing?"

Her attempt to change the subject worked a little too well as she saw Ms. May's face light up.

"Libby is an outstanding member of Mr. Smith's class. She excels not only in her class, but in her grade level. I know we've discussed it before, but she is a good candidate for academic acceleration. She exceeds what second grade has to offer."

Not again. This woman doesn't listen.

Pasting what she hoped was a pleasant expression on her face, Tasha said, "We have discussed this before. I don't feel comfortable moving Libby up a grade. Libby and Blake are twins. I have to consider the dynamics between them. Blake isn't ready to move up, and Libby isn't bored. A move would cause more problems."

"I disagree. Down the road, you'll realize you made the wrong decision." Ms. May paused. "To be honest, you've already made quite a few bad ones."

Tasha bit her tongue in shock. Ms. May never minced words, but to say Tasha was wrong to her face seemed unprofessional. Or rude. Or both. Tasha wasn't even sure what to say. Before she could figure out a comeback, Ms. May continued.

"I do have one other thing to discuss. I got an email from Ms. Shaw about Mr. Gerome's custody rights and what to do if he comes to school asking about the children." The frown reappeared on Ms. May's face. "Am I to expect trouble at my school? Because as you know, I have more than your children to worry about."

Tasha's patience snapped. She didn't know why this woman was being so difficult, nor did she care at this point. Tasha just wanted out of the principal's office.

"I don't know what to expect. Sara gave you a heads up that Doug has no legal rights to take the kids from school." Tasha voice got louder. "Under no circumstances is he to contact the children here. Is that understood?"

Tasha watched Ms. May's face freeze into an unreadable mask. Tasha realized she crossed a line, but she wanted the woman to understand the seriousness of the situation.

"Yes. It is understood. Thank you for your time, Ms. Gerome. I hope we won't need to speak again anytime soon." Ms. May looked down at her desk, signaling the end of the conversation.

Tasha got to her feet. She walked to the door and turned back to see Ms. May going through papers on her desk. Normally, Tasha would walk out of the room to avoid a confrontation. But now she knew if she didn't set Ms. May straight now, she'd never respect her. She doubted the woman would change her mind, but Tasha knew she needed to stand up for herself. It was now or never.

Tasha cleared her throat, and Ms. May looked up.

"I don't know what your issue is, but Blake and Libby are good kids, and I'm a good mother. Nothing Blake drew was inappropriate. You jumped to conclusions, and that's your problem. Libby is fine where she is. And you can deal with my attorney if you let Doug around the kids. I make the best decisions I can. I don't appreciate your judgment."

Without waiting for a response, Tasha walked out of Ms. May's office. She didn't slow down until she got to her minivan. Her hands were shaking as she tried to put the key in the ignition. Realizing she should calm down before driving, Tasha dropped the keys in her lap and rested her head on the steering wheel. She didn't think she could take any more drama in her life.

"Things will get better," she said to herself. "I can do this. Nothing else bad will happen."

She hoped she was right.

26

"I cannot believe that woman. Of all the hurtful things she could have said, she accuses me of being a bad parent because she misunderstands a seven-year-old's drawing." Tasha cradled the phone on her shoulder as she slammed her laundry basket down on the cabinet. "What kind of administrator is she? I don't get it."

"What was that noise? It sounded like something broke," said Helene.

"It was the laundry basket hitting the cabinet. I'm folding clothes." It aggravated Tasha her mother was more concerned over a noise than her grandson. "Were you not paying attention to what I just told you? Ms. May and Mrs. Anderson are out to get Blake."

"Hold on a minute. What happened to your method of dumping the clothes on the floor and picking out what you need from there?"

While she knew she deserved the remark, Tasha bit her tongue to keep from responding. She didn't want to admit folding clothes and putting them away where they belonged wasn't as hard as she thought it was.

"Can we focus on the bigger issue please?" Tasha put several unmatched socks to the side and folded a pair of Blake's shorts. "Like why the principal and teacher are targeting Blake."

"Personally, I'd like to discuss this strange laundry thing that you're doing, but I suppose we can talk about Ina and Cybil. You do realize those ladies are doing what they've always done."

"And just what is it, Mother?" Tasha hoped her mom caught her sarcastic tone. "If you ask me, they're being unfair and cruel."

"A better word for it is nosy. Natasha, think about what happened on Sunday. The entire town heard what Doug did. Of course, people are going to be curious." Tasha stacked Libby's folded pajamas neatly as she listened to her mother. "Plus, Brad was at the game. People saw an eligible bachelor at his nephew's soccer game with his ex-sister-in-law. If I didn't know what was really going on, I'd jump to the same conclusion as Ina May."

"Fine. I'll buy that logic. But it doesn't explain Mrs. Anderson," said Tasha as she folded a pair of Libby's underwear. "Why make a big deal about the picture?"

She heard her mother sigh.

Great. I'm in for another lecture.

"Dear, if you paid attention to the social scene in town, you would know that Cybil Anderson's been trying for years to marry her daughter off. The poor girl still lives at home, and Cybil wants her out. The rumor is Cybil plans to turn her daughter's room into a pottery studio. She thinks you're standing in the way of that."

Tasha loaded the laundry basket with the clean clothes and leaned back against the counter.

"I wonder what she would say if she knew Carlton was the roadblock."

Not realizing the question was hypothetical, her mother answered.

"Oh, Cybil doesn't care. She's as open-minded as I am. The only thing that will upset her is her pottery studio has to wait."

Before she could respond, Tasha heard the beep indicating another call was coming in. She glanced at the caller ID.

"Mom. I've got to go. Sara's calling me."

"I hope she's got good news. Maybe she cleared up the Dr. Purdue review thing."

Pleased by her mother's optimism, Tasha smiled and said, "That would be great."

"Or she could be calling about Doug! Maybe she set up the meeting with him." Tasha's smile vanished. "And don't forget. You have your second speed dating session on Saturday night. Your dad and I are treating the kids to ice skating while you're out."

Tasha groaned. She couldn't believe she'd let her mother talk her into another session. The last thing she wanted to do was spend another depressing evening with men who didn't want to talk to her.

"I don't know. I didn't get anything out of the first time." Tasha took a deep breath before she broke the news to her mother. "I think I'll skip it. You can still take the kids though."

"I told your father you would do this. I even had a backup plan," said Helene triumphantly. "I asked your sister to go. Unfortunately, she said she was busy."

"Since when is Sara busy on a Saturday night?"

"She said something about meeting Yoga Guy for drinks," said Helene.

Tasha's mouth dropped open. "Who or what is Yoga Guy? I didn't know she was dating anyone."

"I think it's someone from her yoga class. It sort of slipped out. That's not something she normally shares with me," said Helene. "Back to the point: You're still going. With Doug back in town, you need to show him you aren't sitting around, pining for him."

"Pining for him? What are you talking about? I'm not pining for anyone."

"You know what I mean. This week will be better," said her mom. "You know what to expect."

"Watching a bunch of desperate women fight over guys who bedazzle their jeans? Yeah, I know what to expect. Sounds like a great evening to me." Tasha's phone beeped again. "Hey, I need to answer Sara."

"Okay. Tell her I love her," said Helene, "and give the kids kisses for me."

"I will." She disconnected with her mother and clicked over to her sister. "Hey, Sara. How are you?"

"Great. And you will be too when you hear what I have to tell you."

Tasha cradled the phone on her shoulder as she hoisted the laundry basket and started to deliver clean clothes throughout the house.

"Well, I could use some good news. What's up?"

"You're cleared from the Dr. Purdue review fiasco."

The news caught Tasha by surprise, and the laundry basket fell to the floor with a thud. The freshly folded clothes dumped onto the ground. Tasha sat down next to them and stared at the mess.

"Crap. I have to start over."

"Start over with what?" Sara asked. "Did you hear what I said?"

"I heard. I'm off the hook with Dr. Purdue."

"Then why don't I hear any excitement in your voice? You should be thrilled. A former employee confessed to tanking the doctor's reputation." Tasha started to tell her sister she was, but Sara kept talking. "Judith Johnson accessed the office's computer system and pulled a list of patient names. She's been using them to write fake reviews since she got fired. You just happened to get caught up in the mess."

Tasha carefully picked up the items that remained folded and put them back in the basket.

"That would be Nurse Judi, all right. The woman was not a pleasant person. Well, that's one less thing I need to worry about. If only I could get these clothes refolded, I'd be on a roll."

When her sister didn't respond, Tasha asked, "You still there?"

"Did you just say you were folding clothes?"

Tasha imagined the look that had to be on her sister's face, and she smiled.

"Yes, I did. Do you have a problem with that?"

"No. Not at all. I only wish you picked up the habit when we still shared a bedroom. I guess now is better than never."

With the basket repacked, Tasha stood up and continued on her way.

"Not to take away from this positive news, but did Doug ever call?" Tasha asked. "I thought we would have heard from him by now."

"So did I. I called his lawyer, but he hadn't heard from him in a while. All I really got out of him is that Doug's not paying his bills."

Tasha slid Blake's clothes into his chest of drawers.

"Should I offer to pay so we can get what we need?"

"Absolutely not!" Tasha winced at the tone of her sister's voice. "You are not going to give that man a thing. Which reminds me, when he does call, you need to give a clear no on the bounce house proposal."

"I know." She walked to Libby's room and put the rest of the clothes away before sitting on her daughter's bed. "I'm surprised no one's heard from him though. It's Tuesday. Two days shows a lot of restraint on his part."

"Let's hope he left town." Sara paused. "You need to be careful. It's no secret I don't like Doug. But, Tasha, the man isn't being rational. I don't want to see you or the kids get hurt."

Tasha started to argue but stopped. The need to defend her ex-husband wasn't there.

Well, that's progress.

"Okay. I will," said Tasha before she changed the subject. "So, who's Yoga Guy?"

She didn't know if it was the fact she didn't argue with her sister or if she caught Sara off guard. Whatever the reason, Tasha grinned as Sara cleared her throat before responding.

"Who told you about that?"

"Mom. I thought you might want to go to speed dating Saturday night, but it sounds like you have plans." When Sara didn't respond, Tasha filled the silence. "Since you have to miss out Saturday, would you be interested in joining us for Libby's piano recital on Sunday? I know she would love to have you there." Just to see what Sara would say, Tasha added, "You can bring Yoga Guy."

"I hate you. Email me the time and location, and I'll be there. Call me if you need me."

Before Tasha could say anything else, her sister hung up. Tasha burst out laughing as she picked up the laundry basket. It was nice to know she could still get under Sara's skin.

27

As Tasha made her way back to the laundry room, her phone alarm went off. The kids would be home soon. It surprised Tasha how fast the day went when she kept up with her chores. Putting things in their rightful spots made things easier. Maybe the new housecleaner Sunshine would last more than a couple of months.

She walked through the kitchen. The counter was clear of everything except a vase of freesias. The sink sparkled. One neat pile of mail sat on the breakfast table. Tasha decided to reward herself with a glass of iced tea before the kids got home. As the ice clinked against the glass, the doorbell rang.

"What did I forget today?" Tasha put the glass down and checked the calendar she now kept on her cell phone. Nothing scheduled. The doorbell rang several times in a row, like someone was holding the button. Wondering who would be in such a rush, she poked her head around the corner. As quickly as she could, she pulled back into the kitchen.

"Damn it, Doug! Why did you have to come here?" Tasha closed her eyes.

What do I do now? He should not be here. Think, Natasha. Think.

Opening her eyes, she heard the third peal of the doorbell as she considered her options. No reason to involve her parents. Brad would drop everything to help, but that would really irritate Doug. Since she knew her sister was sitting in the office, Tasha tapped out a quick text to Sara.

Doug's here. Going to talk to him. Call me in five minutes to make sure all okay.

Not waiting for a response, Tasha tucked the phone in her pocket and peeked out the window by the front door. Doug sat on the bottom step of the porch looking out on the street. She considered going back to the kitchen and hiding, but that wasn't going to make him go away.

Tasha grabbed the house key hanging by the front door and shoved it in her pocket. She opened the door and before Doug turned his head, pulled it closed and locked it as her phone vibrated in her pocket. Without looking, she knew it was Sara. *So much for five minutes.*

"Do you leave all of your house guests waiting at the door?" Doug asked. He stayed seated but twisted his body around to look at her. "It's impolite."

"Look who's calling who impolite."

The words surprised both her and Doug. A half-smile crossed Doug's face as he said, "Well. Someone grew a set. Took you long enough."

Her phone buzzed again, but she ignored it.

"What are you doing here, Doug? You were supposed to call Sara and set up a meeting. I have nothing to say to you."

"Actually, we have a lot to talk about." Doug leaned back and stretched his legs out in front of him as if his visit was an everyday occurrence. "You owe me an answer on that business proposal."

Steeling herself for the argument that was bound to happen, Tasha said, "No. I'm not going into business with you. I'm not giving you any money either." She relaxed a bit when Doug didn't react but kept her distance. "Now, if that's all, I'd like you to leave."

Doug shook his head but didn't speak. Tasha noticed how his overgrown hair brushed against his collar. His physical appearance worried her, but the buzz of her phone kept her from studying him too much. She pulled it out of her pocket and read the text from her sister.

I called the police. They will be there soon. Are you okay?

Tasha winced. Doug wouldn't be happy if the police showed up, but Sara did what she thought best. Tasha glanced up to see what Doug was doing, but he continued to sit there, still shaking his head. She texted a quick *okay* to her sister and returned the phone to her pocket. Trying to decide how best to convince Doug to leave, Tasha cleared her throat.

"Did you hear what I said?" Tasha asked. "You need to leave."

Doug pulled his legs up to the step and propped his elbows on his knees.

"Not until you tell me the truth."

Her eyes narrowed.

"I told you the truth. I'm not giving you any money."

One of his elbows slipped off his knee, throwing him to one side. He fell toward the porch railing but caught himself right before he hit. He pushed back into a sitting position, wobbling a bit as he righted himself. Something about his behavior was off, but Tasha couldn't pinpoint what it was. She walked to the far side of the porch and waited.

"You might change your mind," Doug said.

"No, I won't."

"You will when I ask you what Brad was doing here Sunday night."

Tasha froze.

What the hell? He's spying on me now!

"Can't deny it, can you? So, are you gonna tell me or should I tell you? I think I have a pretty good idea."

Tasha's heart raced. Her phone buzzed again, but she kept her eyes on Doug. He didn't move. He sat there, looking at the road. Positioning herself as close to the porch rail as possible, Tasha remained silent and waited.

"I think you missed me so much, you decided to take the next best thing. Never should have done it." Doug took a deep breath and reached for the rail. Tasha saw it took a lot of effort for him to stand. When he let go of the rail, he swayed backward and for a minute, Tasha thought he was going to fall down the steps. Doug grabbed the porch railing, though and steadied himself.

He's drunk. It's the middle of the afternoon and the man is drunk.

"Doug, I don't know what's going on with you, and I don't care. But you should know the police are on their way."

He took the two steps onto the porch and fell forward, landing on his knees. Tasha held her breath as he struggled to get to his feet. When his efforts failed, he crawled to the front door and pulled himself up using the door handle. Doug fiddled with the handle a couple of times before he turned to Tasha.

"I'm getting my money, then I'm leaving. Why do you have to make things so difficult?"

She watched as he turned back to the door. If her heart wasn't threatening to beat through her chest, the sight would have been funny. He attempted to turn the handle, not realizing it was locked. Doug looked down at his hand as if something were wrong with him. Propping herself on the rail, Tasha swung one leg over the side, just in case Doug attacked her when he realized the door was locked.

But that never happened. Instead, it was as if Doug forgot she was standing there. He put his forehead on the door in frustration. She heard him mumble something as he tapped his head against the wood. As quickly as it started, Doug pushed himself away from the door and turned. Tasha swung her other leg over the rail, ready to jump down if he came at her, but instead, he stumbled down the front porch steps. She watched him weave down the sidewalk and wobble toward the red sports car he'd been driving on Sunday. Without looking back, Doug opened the car door and slid behind the wheel.

Before she knew what she was doing, Tasha called out, "You can't drive when you've been drinking. You'll hurt—"

The car door slammed shut, cutting off her words. She watched in horror as the engine revved, and the car lurched forward. Tasha walked to the front of the porch in time to see Doug turn at the end of the block.

"Someone." Tasha finished her sentence as she sat down on the porch steps. The shock of what just happened drained what remained of her courage, and Tasha began to shake. "It's okay. Nothing happened. He's gone." She repeated the words several times and took slow, steady breaths to compose herself. When she felt calm enough, she picked up the phone and called her sister.

Sara answered the phone before the first ring finished.

"Are you okay? Did the police get there? What did he want? Do you want me to come over?"

Tasha managed a smile at her sister's concern.

"Yes, I'm fine. The police never showed though. Can I come to your office? I don't want to be here at the house alone with the kids until we figure something out." Tasha swallowed her fear. "He's been spying on me, Sara. He saw Brad here the other night after the soccer game and thinks there's something going on between us. Can you imagine that?"

"Come on over. We'll talk when you get here."

The call ended, and for the second time in a week, Tasha was grateful for her sister.

28

Brad sorted through the hospital blueprints on his desk. Everything was progressing well. The approved building permits arrived today, and the contractors were on schedule. Barring any major issues, the renovations would be completed early.

While he was pleased with the progress on the hospital, Brad worried about Tasha. When he talked to her yesterday, she still hadn't heard from Doug. He hadn't called Sara either. He hoped the old adage, no news is good news, applied to this situation, but he knew nothing with his brother was that simple.

Focusing back on his work, he prepared to head to the site for a late afternoon meeting with the supervisor when the receptionist called.

"You have a visitor. Do you have time?"

Brad wasn't expecting anyone, but sometimes his contractors dropped in. A quick glance at the clock told him he had a few minutes to spare, so he told the receptionist to send the visitor through. He gathered the papers on his desk, sliding them into his briefcase. Brad looked up when someone bumped into his door frame.

Doug steadied himself and then walked into his office.

"Guess I should have asked who was here." Brad grimaced as he watched his brother stumble into the room.

"I woulda lied." Doug flopped into a chair. "New receptionist since the last time I was here. What happened to the other one? Did ya sleep with her?"

It was just like Doug to assume everyone had his morals.

"What do you want? I have a meeting."

"You always were direct and to the point," said Doug, propping his feet up on Brad's desk. "I want to know what you're doing with my ex-wife and my kid."

Brad frowned. He thought his brother would ask for money, based on previous events. He didn't expect Doug to bother with Tasha and the kids. Maybe Doug was trying a different angle. Something didn't feel right about the situation, but Brad played along.

"Operative word is 'ex' in that sentence." Brad relaxed back into his chair. "What do you think I'm doing? I'm helping Tasha when I can. I am being the kids' uncle. You're not around, so what do you care?"

His brother's face turned red. Brad knew he needed to be careful since Doug's face only got red when he got angry. Or drinking. If Doug was loaded, Brad knew he should be careful what he said. Anything could set his brother off when he was drunk. Doug's voice interrupted his thoughts.

"Define 'helping' Tasha."

Brad stared at his brother. "What is that supposed to mean?"

"You know what I mean. Are you helping her, say, in the kitchen? Or the garage? Or the bedroom?"

"Damn it, Doug." Brad stood up. "What the hell is your problem?"

"I saw you looking at her at the soccer game. I don't miss a thing."

Brad knew how much Doug had missed. He wasn't about to bring his brother up to speed. Rather than argue, he waited. He knew his brother couldn't stand the silence.

"I know your tricks. And I know what I saw. You and Tasha are doing something. And you do remember she's not supposed to contact you, right?"

"She didn't. I did."

Doug's face got redder. His feet hit the floor, and he leaned forward, putting his forearms on Brad's desk. Brad got a close up view of his brother's bloodshot eyes and frowned.

"What's wrong with your eyes?"

Doug pushed back from the desk, causing the chair to tilt backward. He flailed about before leaning forward. The chair landed on all four legs with a thump.

"I'm asking the questions. And I want to know what's going on. The only reason I can think of is so you can have sex with her. And for the record, it ain't that good."

Now it was Brad's turn to control his temper. He knew everything out of his brother's mouth was a lie and meant to hurt, but it pained him to hear Doug talk about Tasha like that. Brad forced his fists to relax. Getting upset didn't help Tasha, the kids, or himself.

"I meant exactly what I said. Your ex-wife needed some help with the kids. She's a single mom, in case you forgot," Brad said. "The kids missed me, and I missed them. It worked out well."

"You can't help my family unless I say you can."

"They're not your family anymore. And the last time I checked you don't have the right to tell me what to do."

Doug sat back and smiled.

"Sounds like you want her, don't you?"

"God, Doug. You're sick. And from the look of things, drunk

as well." Brad grabbed his briefcase. "Get out of my office. I have things to do."

"I'll leave when I'm ready." Doug stood up. "You want her, and you want my kid. Fine. Well, today is your lucky day. You can have them."

Brad froze. The conversation got worse by the second. He knew he wasn't going to like whatever answer Doug had for his next question.

"What are you talking about now?" said Brad. "They're not yours to give. Tasha can do what she wants."

"Not if I stick around. I can make things harder for Tasha and Blake. You saw what I can do."

"Scream at your own son? That's not something you should be bragging about, you know? And what about Libby? Are you planning to yell at her, too?"

"She's not mine." The red of Doug's face deepened.

"That's not what the paternity tests say."

"Do you want to hear what I'm offering or not?" Doug slammed his hand down on his brother's desk. "Because I'll walk out of this office, and you won't hear what I have to say. And you will regret it. Trust me. I'll make sure you regret it."

"Stop threatening me. Better yet, go. Leave us all alone. You don't want your family, and they don't need you." Brad hated when Doug tried to intimidate him. It hadn't worked when they were kids, and it didn't work now. "You're a bad husband and father. Move on with your life."

"I told you. I'm done with them. All of them. I don't need them and don't want them." Doug smiled at his brother. "But you can have them. For a price."

The absurdity of the situation hit Brad. Doug was bribing him. His brother felt so little toward his family he was willing to walk out of their lives again for money. And since Tasha told him no, Doug came to the next available person—his brother.

"I have to leave. I'm not giving you any money." Brad walked around his desk toward the door. "You're in enough trouble as it is. Leave. Go back to your girlfriend."

Doug stood up, blocking his brother's way.

"I don't think you understand. I want a million dollars, and I'm not leaving town until I get it."

"No, you don't understand. You gave up your family years ago. How you could walk away from them is beyond me, but you did. Just because you're broke now doesn't mean you get to manipulate me or Tasha or anyone else. I'm not giving you money. Tasha's not giving you money. Go away."

Doug held his ground. He leaned in so close Brad smelled the alcohol on his breath.

"I'm not going away until I get what's mine. I can make you give me money, I promise you. You don't give me credit for all the things I'm capable of doing."

Hearing his brother talk like this made Brad sick. He was scared for Tasha and the kids. He was sad he was related to a human being like this. Brad never imagined his brother would go this far for money.

"Get out. You are not welcome here." Brad maneuvered around his brother and put his hand on the door. "Don't come back."

Doug stared at his brother. His face wasn't as red as it had been, which concerned Brad. If he wasn't mad, then what was he? He knew how to deal with Doug's temper, but his schemes were an entirely different matter.

Doug walked slowly past his brother but stopped in the hallway, he turned back and stepped close then leaned in, their faces inches apart.

"You'll regret this. I gave you a chance, and you said no. I won't ask nicely again."

Without another word, Doug turned, hitting the wall again. He pushed himself to the middle of the hallway and shuffled to the lobby. Brad followed a few steps behind. As soon as Doug was out the door, Brad locked the office door and turned back to his receptionist.

"That man is never allowed in here again. If he comes, you need to call 911." Brad nodded toward the door. "I want you to call it a day. I have a meeting, and I don't want you here alone if he decides to come back."

"But I need the hours," said the receptionist. "I know self-defense, and I have pepper spray."

"I'll pay you for the rest of the afternoon. Just go home and be safe."

Brad walked back to his office and picked up the phone. It looked like his afternoon meeting plans had changed.

29

Sara's office buzzed with activity. She'd never seen so many people wedged into the room before. Her niece and nephew sat on the floor around her sand Zen garden. They'd fought over the one rake that came with the set until Sara found an old eyelash comb in her desk. Thrilled to have a make-up brush, Libby created intricate designs that Blake swept away with the rake.

Her mother and father sat on the couch, talking with Bill. He'd taken one look at her face when her parents burst into the office after hearing about Doug's visit and kept them busy so she wouldn't have to deal with their questions.

Tasha and a police officer sat in the chairs opposite her desk. Sara expected her sister to be upset, but instead, Tasha was calm and composed. She answered the officer's questions without shedding a tear and made several suggestions on how to find Doug.

She's finally got herself together. Good for her.

"So, what do we do next?"

The question caught her off guard. She glanced up and saw Tasha and the police officer looking at her.

Clearing her throat, Sara stalled for time. She hadn't been paying attention to the conversation, so she wasn't sure how to answer the question. Her mother took her hesitation as an invitation to interrupt.

"If you ask me, Doug needs to be tracked and brought in. It's not safe for my daughter and grandchildren to go home with him running loose."

"Can we ride along with the police, Grandma?" Blake asked, the rake still in his hand. "Like they do on that live TV show we watch at your house?"

Sara saw Tasha glare at Helene.

"Mom, that show is rated for teenagers. Do not let them watch that stuff." Turning to her son, Tasha said, "No honey, you cannot go on a ride-along. The police can handle it on their own."

Groaning with disappointment, Blake returned to raking sand.

The police officer said, "There isn't much we can do. Mr. Gerome hasn't done anything wrong."

"He's driving while intoxicated. That's illegal the last time I checked," said Tasha. "Why can't you do something about that?"

"If he's still on the road, we'll find him. The sheriff and local law enforcement have been alerted. The only thing I can suggest now is that you and your kids go someplace safe where your ex-husband can't find you. You could file a restraining order as well, but I don't think you have enough evidence for that."

"And it takes too long," said Sara. Her phone rang, and she held up a finger. "Let me get this. Yes, Renee."

"Brad's in the lobby to see you," said Renee. "He said it's urgent. Doug paid him a visit as well. Can I send him back?"

"Yes, please." Sara hung up the phone and looked up to see everyone staring at her. "Brad's here."

"Why?" asked Tasha.

"Doug."

As Sara spoke, Brad appeared in her doorway. A chorus of "Uncle Brad" kept Sara from asking any questions while Libby and Blake hopped up to give their uncle hugs. Sara didn't like the expression on Brad's face, but she quickly forgot about it when she saw who was standing behind Brad.

Yoga Guy.

What the hell is he doing here?

Before she could speak, Tasha stood up and pulled Yoga Guy into an embrace.

"Carlton, what are you doing here?" Tasha asked.

Yoga Guy's name is Carlton?

Sara was surprised when Helene hopped off the couch and inserted herself in the hug. Of course, her mother needed to be in the middle of things.

"Dr. Reynolds, it's nice to see you again. Tasha's back is so much better since you adjusted it. I meant to ask you on Sunday. How do I get an appointment with you? You're always booked."

Yoga Guy is a chiropractor?

"I think I can pull some strings. Just call the office, and I'll get you in," said Carlton. He extricated himself from Helene's arms and smiled at Tasha. "Tasha, how are you? Any pain?"

Sara watched in awe as the man of her dreams stood in her office. She didn't know why he was here, but it was now or never. Clearing her throat, Sara stepped in front of Carlton.

"Hello. We haven't been introduced. I'm Sara Shaw, Tasha's sister, and," Sara nodded toward Helene, "she's my mother."

"It's about time we officially met. I see you at Wednesday night yoga class." Carlton offered his hand. Excited by the prospect of shaking hands with the man she'd been fawning over for the last year, Sara grinned nervously. She took his hand, expecting an explosion of fireworks to signal she finally found her man when Carlton said, "I'm Brad's boyfriend."

Yoga Guy is gay?

The fireworks fizzled as Sara struggled to keep the grin on her lips. Using her best courtroom manners, Sara swallowed her disappointment and pumped Carlton's hand up and down. The look on his face told her she was overcompensating, so she let go of his hand mid-shake. With as much sincerity as she could muster, she said, "It's a pleasure to meet you."

A buzz of disappointment filled Sara's head, blocking out whatever Carlton said.

I am such an idiot. How did I not know I was lusting over a gay man? And am I the only one who didn't know about Brad?

Looking around the room, Sara observed no one else seemed surprised by Carlton's statement. She did notice Helene and Tasha looking at her, like they were waiting for her to say something. Not wanting to deal with her mother or sister, Sara started back to her desk. She could hide behind her computer while she figured out what to do next. As she turned though, someone tugged at her arm.

"I need to talk to you. Alone," said Brad.

Without waiting for her response, Brad pulled her into the hallway. He shut the door behind him. Before she could speak, words tumbled from Brad's mouth.

"Doug showed up in my office. He was drunk, but he tried to blackmail me. He told me if I gave him a million dollars, I could have Tasha and the kids. What a dumbass." Brad ran a hand through his hair before he frowned. "What's wrong with you? You look like you saw a ghost."

"Having Carlton in my office surprised me," Sara said, hoping a vague explanation would suffice. "It's always odd to see someone out of context."

Brad's hand stopped on the top of his head.

"Where have you seen him before?"

A tingle ran down Sara's spine. There was no way Carlton or Brad knew about her little crush, but for some reason Brad's question made her choose her words carefully. "We go to the same yoga studio."

Nodding slowly, a questioning look covered Brad's face.

"So Tasha didn't tell you?"

"Tell me what?" Her eyebrows furrowed together. If she kept getting surprises, Sara might have to break down and get Botoxed. She was too young to have a wrinkled forehead.

"I would have liked to do this under other circumstances, but to expedite the situation, here goes." Brad took both of her hands in his. "Sara, I'm gay. Carlton is my boyfriend."

Relieved she didn't have to process another bombshell, Sara opened her mouth to speak but no words came out. Feeling, and possibly looking, like a fish out of water, she closed her mouth and nodded at Brad before trying again.

"I know. Carlton told me."

"Oh. Okay, then. I guess that's all for the best because we need to focus on Doug and what he's doing," said Brad, before he dropped her hands. "Wait a minute. Why is your entire family here?"

For once, grateful for Doug's stupid behavior, she said, "Doug stopped at Tasha's house. Apparently right before he came to your office." Sara felt better focusing on something she could control. It felt better than thinking about the demise of her imaginary dating life. For now, she had work to do. "He wanted money from her, too."

"There's a police officer in there. Did Doug hurt Tasha or the kids?"

Shaking her head, she leaned against the wall.

"No one got hurt. Doug showed up at Tasha's without warning. I erred on the side of caution and alerted the police. Tasha said he was drunk, and he stumbled up the porch steps." As she started to tell Brad the rest of the story, the irony of the situation dawned on her. "Brad, Doug thinks you and Tasha are having an affair."

Brad shrugged.

"I know. He accused me of the same thing."

"So he doesn't know about Carlton?"

Brad shook his head. "My parents don't know either. Helene and Max found out at the soccer game and I told Tasha Sunday night. Doug doesn't have a clue. So what next?"

Sara straightened up. "Doug didn't do anything to Tasha. The only thing the police can do is arrest him for driving while intoxicated. That is if they find him before he sobers up."

The door to Sara's office flung open, and the police officer rushed out.

"Just got a call from dispatch. A red sports car wrapped itself around a giant oak tree. Car matches the description of the one Mr. Gerome is driving. I'll be in contact once I have more details."

30

"Do we get to see him in the hospital?" Blake asked. "We visited Grandma when she got her gold bladder out."

"It's a gall bladder, silly. Don't you know anything?" Libby frowned at her brother before looking at Tasha. "I don't want to go to the hospital. It smells funny. Plus, Grandma said Daddy's injuries were self-inflicted. So why do we have to go if it's his fault?"

Tasha looked at Blake and Libby sitting on the couch. She'd brought them home as soon as the police confirmed Doug was alive, but waited until after dinner to tell the kids about Doug's accident.

"I won't make you go, Libby, but this is probably the last time you'll see him for a while." Tasha debated how much to tell the kids. The paramedics credited his over-the-limit blood alcohol level for saving his life. He was so out of it, his body didn't tense up when the crash occurred. He didn't have any life-threatening injuries. Broken ribs, cracked tibia, face lacerations, and miscellaneous bruises would slow him down, though. So would the trip to jail. She settled on a partial truth. "He'll be leaving town as soon as he is out of the hospital."

Blake shook his head. "Mommy, he's not leaving town. He's going to jail. Grandma told me so!"

Of course. Why wouldn't she tell them?

"She said he was sauced," Libby said. "What does that mean?"

And it gets better.

Before Blake could share any more of his grandmother's wisdom, Tasha answered Libby.

"It means he was drunk. It's illegal to drink alcohol before you drive. It makes you do bad things."

Libby frowned. "Like run into a tree?"

Who has conversations like this with seven-year olds?

"Yes, like run into a tree." She turned to Blake. "After Daddy gets better, he'll go to another town where the jail is."

The kids looked at each other. Tasha expected tears or some other show of emotion. Instead, Blake and Libby shrugged.

"We don't see him much anyway," said Libby.

Blake nodded. "All he does is yell at me. Maybe he'll learn manners in jail."

She kept her face neutral. There was no chance in hell that Doug would come out of jail nicer than when he went in, but she wasn't telling the kids that. Her mother would, but not her.

Changing the subject, Tasha asked, "Okay. Since that's decided, what do you think of Aunt Sara babysitting this weekend?"

"Why can't Uncle Brad? He's fun," said Blake. He stood, walked to where she was sitting and crawled into Tasha's lap. Touched by the fact he wanted to be close to her, Tasha gave her son a kiss on the top of his head. "I bet he'd make cookies with us again."

Libby followed her brother's lead. She elbowed Blake. "Scoot over. I want to sit there too." As soon as she was comfortable, Libby said, "Uncle Brad has a social life, Blake. He and Carlton are dating. Aunt Sara is a spinster. She has more time to watch us. Can I have a kiss, too?"

Tasha planted a smooch on Libby's head before she asked, "Let me guess. Grandma told you that, too."

"No." Libby shook her head. "Aunt Sara did."

"What's a spinster?" asked Blake. "Is it like a gangster?"

Tasha felt Libby elbow her brother again.

"Really Blake? Don't you learn anything in Mrs. Anderson's class?"

Blake hopped off her lap. He scowled as he glared at his sister.

"Yeah, but I don't know all the answers. Mrs. Anderson said that's okay, cuz that's why you go to school." Blake paced in front of her and Libby before he put his hands on his hips. "So what's a spinster?"

Tasha wasn't sure which was better: a conversation about Brad's dating life or Sara's lack thereof.

Sara would be mortified right now.

"A spinster is someone who doesn't get married when her mom thinks she should," said Libby. She looked up at Tasha. "You can't tell me when to get married. I'm going to be a cardio-thoracic surgeon and no man is going to stand in the way of my career."

Tasha bit the inside of her lip to keep from laughing and nodded.

"I wanna be a trash man," said Blake. "They find cool stuff."

Libby grimaced and shook her head.

"Men."

Tasha couldn't help laughing this time.

"So what do you two want to do when Aunt Sara is here?"

"Do you think Uncle Brad and Carlton will get married like Olivia and Oliver's dads did?" Blake asked. Tasha should have known the kids would return to the topic of their uncle. "Will they get divorced, too?"

Once again, her daughter answered Blake's question. "Aunt Sara said not everyone gets divorced. Some people stay married until they die. She doesn't think people take the time to find the right person. And even if they find the right person, sometimes they give up too soon."

"Hold on. When did you have time to talk to Aunt Sara about all this stuff?" Tasha didn't recall seeing Libby and Sara together while they were in her sister's office.

"When you and Grandma argued about where we were spending the night. Aunt Sara let me sit in her chair. She told me everything that was going on."

"Yes, she certainly did, didn't she?"

"Will we call Carlton Uncle Carlton when he marries Uncle Brad?" asked Blake.

"Olivia has to call her stepfather Mr. Robert. She says it sucks. I like Uncle Carlton better," said Libby. "Or Dr. Carlton. Grandma said he is a whiz-bang chiropractor."

As she listened to Libby and Blake debate Carlton's future nickname, Tasha realized how lucky she was. Libby and Blake were two well-adjusted kids despite Doug's shenanigans and her mother's well-intentioned, but irresponsible comments. The teenage years might change things, but for now, her heart felt happy.

It was also nice to know her family had her back. She didn't necessarily agree with her mother or sister telling the kids everything that happened, but it made things easier. Everyone knew the facts. No need to worry about what would happen if someone discovered the truth later on down the line.

The feel of Libby's head on her chest drew Tasha's attention back to the conversation.

"Are you excited to go on a date tomorrow night, Mommy?"

Libby asked. "Grandma said she hopes you get her money's worth."

"Why would Grandma say that?" asked Blake.

Ignoring the questions, Tasha reached out her arm and wiggled her fingers to get Blake to come back to her lap. He slid up next to Libby, and Tasha wrapped her arms around them both.

"I'm excited to spend tonight with the two of you. I love you both," said Tasha. "What do you two say to a game of Go Fish?"

Blake and Libby squirmed out of their mother's grasp.

"First one to get the playing cards, gets to deal," said Blake as he ran out of the room.

Libby followed close on his heels.

"That's not fair. You got a head start."

Tasha smiled. Instead of stewing about Doug or speed dating, she planned to enjoy game night with the kids. And she couldn't wait to hear how her sister rated as a babysitter.

31

Tasha glanced at the mirror in the hotel hallway. She looked like she belonged on the red carpet. Sara was right to suggest she go to the salon. Having someone else do her hair and make-up made her feel glamorous, plus it looked better than her own amateur attempts. Even if the speed dating session sucked, and she assumed it would, her new look made her feel like a million bucks.

Standing up a little bit straighter, Tasha strode to the sign-in table in the lobby. She recognized the check-in woman and the familiar tight red dress and sparkly stilettos. Tasha grinned when she noticed the woman's make-up and hair. They were the same, and the woman was flipping through the same fitness magazine. Tasha hoped their conversation wouldn't be a repeat as well.

The woman smiled when she looked up. This week, her smile made it all the way to her eyes. Tasha returned the smile, confident in her appearance.

Instead of last week's conservative outfit, Tasha wore a black silk wrap dress with strappy, gold sandals. It was one of five outfits her sister had brought over when she came to babysit.

At first, Tasha was skeptical about wearing Sara's clothes. Years of yoga left Sara toned and firm in places where Tasha was pleasantly plump. Tasha didn't see how the clothes could possibly fit her. She nixed the two form-fitting dresses immediately as well as a dress that reminded her of one Helene wore.

"Why did you have to tell me that?" Sara asked when Tasha pointed out the similarities. "Now, I have to get rid of it. And it was expensive."

The process of getting dressed was more fun than Tasha imagined. Sara assured her this dress would turn heads wherever she wore it. Tasha figured she was overdressed compared to the mini-skirts and tank tops from the previous week, but she wasn't comfortable in that sort of outfit. She was conservative and classy, not sequins and flashy.

"So glad you could join us," said the woman. "Is this your first time?"

"No, I was here last week." Tasha started to remind the woman about her AA comment, but decided against it. "I didn't have much luck, so I thought I would try again."

"I can't believe someone like you didn't find a match. You look stunning. I'm sure you'll make a connection tonight. Good luck."

Tasha walked away from the woman in awe. That woman ignored her last week. Now the same woman thought she looked good. Apparently, hair, make-up, and clothes did make the woman. She wandered into the conference room. Identical to last week's set up, Tony stood at his post, reading a magazine. He glanced up as she wandered the room looking for her spot.

"Hey there. Can I help you find your name?" Tony closed his magazine and walked toward her, winking as he approached. "I put all the name tags out so I'm sure I can find it for you."

Tasha grinned. Last time, he paid no attention to her. Tonight, he wanted to help. She continued to be amazed at what a little primping accomplished. Tasha shook her head and picked up her name tag from the table.

"No, I'm right here. I'm fine."

"First timer, huh?" said Tony. "You'll really like it, hon."

Tasha pulled the backing off the name tag and stuck it to her dress. "No, I was here last week. I didn't enjoy it the first time, but I decided to give it another chance."

"No way. I would remember a hottie like you. I musta' been off the night you was here."

"No, you were here. You're the one who told me I couldn't switch seats because of the rules."

"Ah, you insult me! I would never do that." Tony slapped his right palm to his chest, his heart bruised by Tasha's comment. He looked at her name tag, or her cleavage, she couldn't tell which. "Tasha. Beautiful name. No way I'd forget it."

His statement confirmed he was full of crap, but Tasha didn't argue. She didn't want any more of his attention, especially as he was looking down her dress.

"I don't want to hold you up." She saw a couple of women walk in the room, looking uncertain about what to do next. They were dressed like she was the week before, presentable for a PTO meeting, but not a speed dating session. "Looks like you have some more customers. You should go say hello."

Tony shrugged. "They'll figure it out. They look smart enough."

Tilting her head, Tasha frowned. "What do you mean? They look smart enough?"

"Most times when women are dressed like that, it's cuz they're lawyers or accountants or moms." Tony looked Tasha up and down and gave her a low whistle. "Not like you though. You're smokin'."

Tasha started to ask if that was a compliment when one of the women interrupted them.

"Are you in charge here?" the woman asked Tony. Her name tag read Nancy. "This is our first time, and we need some help."

"I'll be with yous in a minute. I'm busy right now," Tony said as Tasha heard someone call her name.

"Tasha, is that you?" She turned to the voice and saw Greg, Blake's soccer coach, walking towards her. She felt her cheeks flush a little when she saw his double take at her appearance. Thankful to leave Tony behind, she started toward Greg. Tasha stopped in front of him and he said, "Wow, you look fantastic."

"Thank you. Nice to see you here." Greg surprised her with a brief hug and peck on the cheek. As they parted, Tasha realized while Greg looked good in his coach's T-shirt and athletic shorts, he looked better in a sports coat and jeans. "Do you come here often?"

Tasha cringed at her word choice, but Greg didn't seem to notice.

"No, this is my first time. Thought I'd try something new." Greg paused as if considering something. "To be honest, my mom signed me up. She wants grandkids, and she thinks I'm taking too long. Embarrassing, huh?"

Tasha let out a belly laugh.

"My mother sent me here too, so I can relate."

Greg looked around the room. "So how does this thing work?"

"Well, you find your name tag on a table, and when Tony says go, you start dating." Tasha made rabbit ears with her fingers when she said the word dating. "Then you switch tables when he says so. I have to warn you: this is not for the faint-hearted. Last week was pretty ugly."

Greg looked over at Tony and Nancy, who were now having a heated conversation about seating assignments.

"It's not looking real good right now, either." Greg shifted his weight from one leg to another then asked Tasha, "So is

Doug still in town? Should I be prepared for a repeat appearance at the next soccer game?"

Tasha hesitated. She didn't want to be the one who told people Doug was recuperating in the hospital from the accident, nor did she want to explain his potential jail time. They would find out soon enough. Instead of giving details, Tasha shook her head.

"No, Doug will not be at another game anytime soon."

"Good to know. Blake played great the rest of the game, but I know he was upset. How about you? Are you okay?"

"I'm good. Thanks for asking." Greg's question surprised Tasha, but she liked the fact he cared enough to ask. "It's been quite the week, but we're all okay."

Raised voices interrupted them. Tony and Nancy's conversation morphed into an argument. A crowd circled around the two as Nancy shook her finger in Tony's face. Tony responded with several rude comments about Nancy's outfit, which resulted in Nancy's finger jabbing into Tony's chest.

Another man, who Tasha recognized as Jim from her last session, called out, "I bet $5 the broad slaps him. Who's in?" Voices, both male and female, erupted in response.

"Wow, this evening is pretty colorful, and the dating hasn't even started," said Greg. "I'm not sure this is what my mother expected when she signed me up."

Tasha nodded her agreement and made a quick decision.

"At the risk of upsetting your mother, would you like to get a drink with me instead of hanging out here? We can go to the hotel bar. I have a feeling the session may be delayed." Tasha gestured at the cluster of people who were now making bets on the outcome of the conversation. "I don't need to see how this ends."

Greg's face broke into a big smile. "Are you kidding? That sounds great. Let's not tell my mom!"

Laughing, Greg and Tasha slipped out of the room.

32

As quietly as possible, Tasha slid her key into the front door lock. She'd texted Sara to let her know she was grabbing a drink with Greg, but she was later than she'd planned. One drink turned into two, so she opted for a ride-share home after she insisted Greg do the same.

The door opened, and she let herself in. Tasha gently placed her keys and purse on the entry table, then sighed in relief as she stepped out of the gold sandals she'd worn all night. The shoes might make the outfit, but they killed her feet.

"Dear God, I'm too old for this crap," she said as she bent down to massage her throbbing foot.

"Too old for what?" Tasha looked up to see her sister standing in the kitchen doorway. Sara tapped her wrist where a watch might have been. "A little bit late, don't you think?"

Rolling her eyes, Tasha continued rubbing her foot.

"Hi, Mom. You didn't need to stay up and wait for me."

She laughed at the unhappy expression on her sister's face.

"Do not call me Mom. That is insulting."

"I know. That's why I said it."

Sara turned back into the kitchen, and Tasha followed. She pointed to the board game sitting on the kitchen counter.

"How did that go?"

Her sister took a glass out of the cabinet, filled it with water, and handed it to Tasha.

"I lost every single game. And not all of them on purpose. I had no idea Libby is so competitive." Sara dried her hands on the dishtowel before turning to the kitchen table. "I take it you left your minivan at the hotel."

"I'm not *pulling a Doug*. That would be stupid, among other things." Gulping down the water, Tasha nodded. "Other than beating you, how did the kids do? Everyone go to bed on time?"

Sara nodded as she pulled out a chair and sat down.

"No problems from either one of them. Blake wasn't wild about brushing his teeth, but after I pulled up a picture of a toothless kid from the Internet, he changed his tune." She folded her hands in front of her. "They asked a lot of questions about Doug."

Tasha refilled her water glass. Instead of joining her sister at the table, she leaned back against the cabinet and took another sip of water while she waited for Sara to continue, but her sister sat quietly, gazing at the table. Sadness washed over Tasha. She couldn't remember Sara this subdued. Professional, yes. Depressed, no.

Damn it, Doug. You even put Sara in a bad mood.

"Sorry. They've been doing that since the accident." Tasha sipped her water before she asked, "What do you think of me visiting Doug in the hospital?"

When Sara shrugged, Tasha frowned. She'd expected her sister to protest any contact with her ex-husband, but instead Sara sat at the table starring at her hands. Confused she asked, "Are you okay? I know this week was crazy, but you seem quieter than usual. Can I do anything?"

She wasn't sure, but she thought she saw tears in her sister's eyes. Before she could say anything though, Sara stood up from the table and grabbed a few tissues from the box on the counter. She blew her nose after she sat down.

"Stress of the week, I think," said Sara. "Plus my allergies are bothering me."

Tasha picked up the tissue box and brought it to the table. Something told her Sara wasn't telling her the full story, but she wasn't sure how to proceed. She'd spent more time with Sara in the last two weeks and felt closer to her sister than she had in a long time, but they still weren't exactly bosom buddies.

You can do this, Tasha. Just talk to her.

"Yeah. Tell me about it. And you've got all your other cases on top of this mess." When Sara squeezed her eyes closed, Tasha couldn't stand it anymore. She walked to the table and covered Sara's hand with her own. "Is there something else you want to talk about? I'm here for you if you want to talk."

Sara squeezed her hand but continued to sit quietly at the table. Not sure what else to do, Tasha pulled out a chair and joined Sara. She waited, still holding her sister's hand. About the time her hand went numb, Sara released it and said, "You know when you were giving me a hard time about Yoga Guy?"

The change in topic surprised Tasha, but she nodded.

"Yeah, I told you to bring him to Libby's recital tomorrow. Can he make it?"

Pressing her lips together, Sara shook her head.

"He'll be there all right. Just not with me."

The reality of the situation clicked. The man her sister loved was unavailable. The urge to protect her sister bubbled up inside of her.

"I'm sorry, Sara. That sucks," Tasha said, pounding one fist into her palm. Sara rewarded her with a glimmer of a smile. "I can go rough him up if you want me. I know a little something about two-timing men."

"Thank you, but I don't think Brad would appreciate that."

Tasha's fist stopped midway to her fist.

"Why would Brad care?"

Sara looked down at her hands as she spoke.

"Because Yoga Guy is Carlton."

Tasha frowned as she stared at her sister in disbelief.

"Hold on." She shook her head. "You and Carlton were dating before Carlton and Brad got together?"

Sara held up her hands.

"No, nothing like that," said Sara, averting her eyes as she continued. "I wasn't actually dating him."

"What does that mean, exactly?" asked Tasha. "You were flirting with him?"

Her sister sighed and looked up. Tasha studied her sister's face for some clue as to how she was feeling. Gone were the tears. Sara didn't look angry. The only thing Tasha could detect was sadness.

"I wanted to flirt with him. I wanted to date him. The problem was I didn't have the guts to talk to him. If I would have actually talked to him, I would have known long ago that he wasn't interested in me. Instead, he walked into my office with Brad." Sara put her head down on the table. "How embarrassing is it to find out that the man you daydream about is gay? And in a relationship with someone who is more or less family?"

Oh my God. She's human after all.

Tasha rubbed her sister's back, not sure what to say. If Sara hadn't been so distraught, laughter might have been the answer, but Tasha knew she wasn't ready to see the humorous side of things. Instead of saying anything, Tasha sat quietly. She hoped her presence was some comfort for Sara.

After a few minutes of comfortable silence, Sara looked up.

"Why would you want to visit Doug in the hospital?"

Clearing her throat, Tasha stood up to refill her water glass.

"I didn't think you heard that."

"Of course I did. Embarrassment doesn't affect my hearing." Sara nodded at the cabinet. "Can you bring me a glass of water, too?"

As she got a second glass down, Tasha considered how to explain her feelings. Tasha hadn't been sure Sara would understand her need for closure with Doug, but Sara's revelation about Yoga Guy/Carlton gave her hope. She filled the glass with water, walked back to the table and placed the glass down in front of her sister.

"I don't know what's wrong with Doug, but I need to tell him he can't do this to me or the kids again. Or to Brad for that matter. Never in our relationship have I stood up for myself. It's about time I did."

"You don't have to," said Sara. "He's in the hospital for a while, then he's looking at jail time."

Tasha nodded.

"Mom told the kids. I didn't know you went to jail for a DUI."

"You do when it's your third one. I can't imagine any judge being lenient in a case like this. I could be wrong, but the likelihood of Doug getting out of this with another slap on the wrist seems slim." Sara looked at the clock on the kitchen wall. "I'm going home. I need some sleep. So do you. Maybe that will give you some clarity."

"Clarity for what?"

"On whether you should visit Doug."

Without waiting for a reply, Sara stood up and headed out of the kitchen. Tasha didn't know why, but she called out, "Hey, Sara?"

Her sister poked her head back in the kitchen.

"Yes?"

Getting out of the chair, Tasha walked over and hugged her. Sara stood as stiff as a board for a few seconds before hugging her back. After a moment, Sara drew back and looked at her.

"What was that for?"

Tasha walked toward the front door.

"Oh, I don't know. Maybe a thank you for being here for me. I know we've had our differences, but I don't think I could have done this without your help."

Sara shrugged.

"I'm sure you could have used a babysitting service tonight. I was just helping out."

Rolling her eyes, Tasha said, "You know what I mean. Not tonight. I mean the stuff with Dr. Purdue and Doug."

"You don't have to thank me. That's what sisters are for. Plus, I'm billing you for it."

Stopping by the entry table, Tasha said, "Of course you are. But I'm being serious. I haven't always been nice to you. I'm beginning to realize how much easier life would have been if I had."

"I left a bit to be desired as well. I could have been more supportive, but I teased you instead." Sara picked up her purse that was sitting on the table. She dug out her keys before she continued. "If you decide to see Doug, I'll go with you."

Teasing her sister, Tasha asked, "Do I need legal representation to go to the hospital?"

Sara grinned back. "No. I'll be there for moral support."

Tasha nodded and let her sister out. She waited until she pulled away from the house before she closed and locked the door. Picking up her shoes and purse, Tasha headed down the hallway to her room, flicking off lights as she went.

Considering everything that happened this week, tonight ended on a good note. Drinks with Greg was unexpected. Her talk with Sara was unprecedented. All that was left was to make a decision about Doug.

33

The sliding doors swooshed open, and Tasha wrinkled her nose as she walked into the hospital. The smell of antiseptic assaulted her nose. Hospitals were never her favorite place. She didn't know if it was because of the smell or what happened in hospitals. Combined with her current mission of putting Doug in his place, her nerves were shot.

I should have taken Sara up on her offer to come with me.

She walked through the foyer and headed to the information desk. Tasha passed a cart full of flowers. A bundle of balloons proclaiming, "It's a Girl!" in hot pink was tied to a vase of white roses and stargazer lilies.

I wonder if there is a balloon that says "Thanks for getting out of my life!"

Shaking the thought from her head, Tasha waited her turn at the desk. Four people stood in front of her so she continued to look around the lobby. An older gentleman pushed a white-haired woman in a wheelchair into the gift shop. A little boy wearing a "I'm a Big Brother" T-shirt clutched a teddy bear while his father carried him onto an elevator. A young woman sat in the corner hunched over her cell phone.

"Next please."

Tasha got Doug's room number and directions to the floor where he was resting. She headed to a bank of elevators when someone bumped into her. The force of the impact caused the bag Tasha carried to fall to the floor. Its contents, a few personal hygiene products and some magazines, scattered on the floor. Tasha bent down to corral the items she'd brought for Doug. It seemed silly now to bring him these things, but she didn't want to show up empty-handed.

"Here. Let me help you." The woman who ran into her bent down, gathering the toothbrush, toothpaste, and deodorant as well as the box of breath mints. As the woman turned to toward her, Tasha did a double take.

"Ms. May. How are you today?"

The look on the principal's face made it clear she wasn't expecting to run into anyone she knew at the hospital. The principal pushed the items at Tasha. "I should have been watching where I was going. I'm in a bit of a hurry."

Not sure what to say, Tasha took the items and tucked them back in her bag, then tapped the elevator call button. Ms. May waited next to her. The awkward silence lasted until a *ding* signaled the elevator's arrival. The doors slid open. Tasha motioned for Ms. May to enter the elevator first, then she followed her. After pressing the button for Doug's floor, Tasha asked, "What floor?"

"Seven please."

After she tapped number for the correct floor, Tasha gazed at the front of the elevator. Ms. May's presence wasn't going to bother her. She'd told the woman several days ago how she felt and nothing said today was going to change that.

Please let this be a quick and quiet ride.

She rolled her eyes when she heard the principal clear her throat.

"I owe you an apology for the other day, Ms. Gerome."

Tasha turned in disbelief. As she looked at the woman, Tasha took in her worried expression. The knuckles on her right hand were white as they clutched several magazines while her left hand smoothed out her suit jacket.

She's nervous about apologizing to me. Who would have thought?

"You were right. I jumped to conclusions. In my position, I know better than to do that, but it seemed like the most obvious explanation. I hope you will accept my apology."

Stunned, Tasha nodded. It felt good to hear someone tell her she was right.

"Of course. Thank you," said Tasha. She paused, not sure if she should continue the conversation. Unsure what to say, Tasha asked, "Who are you visiting, if you don't mind me asking?"

Ms. May's shoulders relaxed when she answered.

"My sister-in-law is in for a knee replacement. Complications kept her over a few nights."

"Nothing serious I hope."

"She'll go to rehab tomorrow, but she's bored and needed something to read." Ms. May held out the magazines she was carrying. Tasha recognized the latest gossip rags. "I typically don't read this type of stuff, but under the circumstances, I thought it was appropriate. I assume you're here to see your ex-husband."

The principal's statement surprised her, though she didn't know why. News about Doug's accident would have spread quickly, and Ms. May kept tabs on her students' families.

Guess it's easier than having to tell her myself.

"I thought I'd come by and bring him a few things." She didn't elaborate seeing as how Ms. May picked them up from the lobby floor. "He'll be here a few days."

"From what I heard, he's lucky to be alive. The alcohol saved him. At least this time."

The elevator dinged, and the doors opened on the seventh floor.

"This is my stop." Ms. May took two steps out before she turned back to Tasha. "Again, I am sorry for my behavior. Please don't let me keep you away from the school. You make a great addition to the PTO Welcoming Committee. Have a good visit."

"You too." Tasha waved as the doors closed. She leaned back on the wall of the elevator. Never in a million years would she ever guess the principal would admit she was wrong. Tasha took it as a good sign. It gave her ego a boost, and she needed it. Standing up to Doug was going to be hard.

The elevator dinged as it reached the ninth floor. Tasha stepped out as the doors opened. She looked for a sign to tell her the way to Doug's room, but all she needed to do was listen.

"You call this food? The mashed potatoes are lumpy and the chicken tastes like the sole of my shoe. Bring me something edible."

As she walked toward Doug's voice, she listened for a response. She heard nothing but, a few seconds later, saw an elderly woman back out of a room pulling a food cart. Tasha hurried to hold the door open for the woman.

"Thank you, dear," said the woman. "I appreciate your help."

"No problem." Tasha started into the room but felt the woman's hand on her arm. She let the door slowly swing closed as she turned back to see what the woman wanted.

"You sure you want to go in there, sweetie? He's not in a good mood."

Tasha smiled.

"I know. I've spent some time with him," said Tasha. "But I'll be okay."

And for the first time since she entered the hospital, Tasha knew she would be fine.

34

Tasha stepped inside the hospital room and stopped. The lights were dim, and the blinds were closed. Except for the patient in the bed, the room appeared unoccupied. No flowers or cards brightened the counter tops. The television was silent. The white board where the nurse monitored the patient's pain levels even seemed depressing.

Doug lay back against a stack of pillows, his eyes shut. Stitches peeked out of a bandage on his right temple and the bluish tinge of a developing bruise covered the right side of his face. A traction device elevated his leg a few inches above the bed. His hands rested on his chest, but she noticed he cringed each time he drew in a breath. The sight of Doug lying in the hospital bed tugged at her heartstrings.

Is it mean of me to tell him to stay out of our lives while he's in pain?

"I can hear you breathing. You damn well better have brought me food that doesn't suck." said Doug without opening his eyes.

No, definitely not mean enough.

"I brought you a toothbrush and deodorant but no food."

His eyes flew open. Tasha caught a flicker of surprise before it was edged out by his signature looks of superiority and disregard.

"Unless you're bringing me a check, you can leave."

Ignoring his request, Tasha walked further into the room. She approached the hospital bed, aware of Doug's scrutiny. She placed the bag of toiletries on his bedside table, then turned to the well-used beige recliner in the corner of the room. Hoping Doug couldn't hear the nervous beating of her heart, Tasha took a deep breath to steady her nerves and sat down.

The vinyl cracked and popped under her weight. Pulling the handle on the side, the footrest lifted up and Tasha settled into the comfortable, if ugly, chair. She placed her hands in her lap and waited. She made it this far. Now, it was Doug's turn.

She didn't have to wait long before Doug's patience snapped.

"What do you want? Did you come by to gloat? Happy I got hurt?"

She shook her head.

"I've never enjoyed seeing someone else in pain. Even you."

"Then you think I'm going to jail and came to say goodbye?" he asked. The left side of his mouth lifted, fixing a twisted smile on his face. "You wasted your time. I'm heading back to St. Thomas next week."

Tasha frowned. Even laid up in a hospital bed, injured by his own irresponsibility, Doug believed he was immune to any consequences to his actions.

"I'm not interested in where you go, Doug. I came by today to set the record straight. I'm finished putting up with all of your crap."

Doug's laughter was cut short when he gasped in pain and grabbed his side. She watched him grimace as he struggled to catch his breath. While she didn't like the fact he was in pain,

Tasha stayed strong in her resolve to show him he had no power over her.

"Pardon me if I can't laugh at your joke." His hand curled protectively over his ribs. "You don't have the guts to be finished with me."

Where once these words would have panicked her, the statement fell away empty and meaningless. Today's visit was for her and her alone. Doug was selfish and would never change. But she didn't need to keep placing herself in his line of fire. She had her kids and her family and maybe even Greg. She didn't need a narcissistic con artist. She stood up when she answered Doug.

"Actually, I do. Life is too short to put up with someone like you. I don't need you. I've tried to be civil for Blake and Libby, but you can't return the favor. So feel free to go back to St. Thomas or wherever it is that you want. We're all good here."

She started to the door when Doug asked, "What's that supposed to mean?"

Staring at the door, Tasha prepared herself for whatever trick Doug had up his sleeve. He wasn't stupid. He understood what she said. So what was he getting at? She didn't bother turning around when she answered.

"I've created a life for myself and the kids, and it no longer includes you. It could have, but you wanted out," said Tasha. She'd debated bringing the kids into the conversation, but since this was the last time she planned to talk to Doug, she knew it was now or never. Turning back to face him, Tasha said, "The kids know what happened."

Doug snorted, then grasped the bed rails in pain.

"Because you told them."

Ignoring the remark, she continued.

"I offered to bring them here to see you today. To find out how you're doing. Neither one of them was interested."

"Blake didn't want to see me?"

The hurt in Doug's voice sounded authentic and his expression was serious for the first time since she entered his room.

"No. He didn't."

"Ungrateful little—"

She promised herself she wouldn't get emotional, but she wasn't going to stand around and let Doug insult her son and ignore her daughter anymore.

"No, Blake is not ungrateful. He's smart," she said. "He sees through you. Libby does, too. Parents are supposed to love their children, not manipulate them. The kids are old enough to understand what you're doing."

"Sure they are. Like I believe you wouldn't twist the facts to make yourself look good."

She repressed the urge to justify all the things she'd done in the past. Tasha thought about the times she defended Doug. The wasted effort spent trying to fix herself in hopes that Doug would want to be with her and the kids. Not until now did it finally click that nothing she did would ever please her ex-husband.

"Goodbye, Doug. I hope you find what you're looking for."

Without waiting for his response, Tasha walked to the hospital room door and opened it. She ignored Doug's angry protests and made her way down the hall. As she turned toward the elevator, she heard his last-ditch attempt to insult her.

"You'll be back. You always come back."

Tasha smiled when she pushed the elevator call button.

"Nope. Not this time."

35

"That was excellent, honey. I never knew takeaway fried chicken tasted better on real plates." Helene sat back and dabbed her mouth. Takeout containers covered Tasha's dining room table, and everyone looked satisfied. "Family dinners are my favorite. We should do this more often."

"It helps when we have something to celebrate," said Max.

Libby looked up in confusion.

"What are we celebrating?"

Tasha answered for her dad.

"Your performance at the piano recital. It was incredible. Wasn't it nice that all of us got to see you play?"

"Soccer games are funner," Blake said.

Libby rolled her eyes at her brother before asking Tasha, "Can I be excused? I want to draw a picture about my piano recital."

"Me too?" Blake asked. "I wanna play with Legos."

Tasha checked her watch.

"Fifteen minutes until bath time. You are excused," Tasha said, then added, "Be sure to take your plates to the kitchen."

Blake grumbled but followed Libby to the kitchen with his

plate. After the kids left the room, Tasha looked around. Helene, Max, Sara, Brad and Carlton finished eating as they chatted about the recital. Grateful for the support around her, Tasha couldn't remember a time when she was happier or more relaxed.

"I hope that smile has something to do with your love life." Her mother's question caught her off guard. "You still haven't told me about Greg yet."

"Mom, do we have to do this now?" Tasha waved at the rest of the people sitting around the table. Everyone was doing the best they could to keep a smile from their faces. Frowning at the group, she said, "No one wants to hear about my dating life."

"I think they do," said Helene. "Go ahead and spill. We aren't going to let you off the hook until you do."

"If it makes you more comfortable, I'll take care of clean up." Carlton stood up and gathered the plates close to his. "Tasha, you deserve a break after the last couple of weeks."

Helene popped to her feet.

"I should help you. You're a guest."

Max put his hand on his wife's shoulder and guided her back into the chair. He grabbed her plate, then his. "Brad and I'll help Carlton, dear. You sit here and enjoy the time with your daughters."

Brad winked at Tasha before he grabbed more dishes and followed Max and Carlton to the kitchen. Helene watched the men leave and turned back to the table. Tasha recognized the smug look on her mother's face—she got what she wanted. Sitting back in her chair, she prepared for her mother's interrogation.

"Thank goodness they're gone. Now tell me exactly what's happening with you and Greg."

Despite the fact that it was none of her mother's business,

Tasha didn't mind sharing this time. The prospect of spending time with Greg was exciting, and she wanted everyone to know.

"We're going out on Saturday."

"Do you know what you're wearing? Where are you going? Who's watching the kids?"

"Mother, leave her alone. If she needs our help, she'll ask." Sara smiled at her sister. "Won't you?"

"Absolutely." Tasha smiled. "You two will be the first people I ask if I need anything. Speaking of which," she turned to her sister, "have you heard anything else about Doug?"

Helene grabbed her hand.

"What do you mean? Is he back?" Helene turned to Sara. "I thought he was going to jail."

Sara shook her head.

"I explained to you there is a legal process to follow. It takes time to work through the system. For the moment though, he's free."

Crossing her arms over her chest, Helene said, "That isn't right. He shouldn't be allowed to wander around. He could hurt someone else."

Her sister started to answer, but Tasha held up her hand. She needed to make sure her mother understood the situation.

"The only person he hurt was himself. There isn't anything we can do about it, Mom. It's out of our hands. He's not going to bother me anymore, though. I was clear about how I felt when I went to the hospital."

Helene threw her hands in the air.

"I still don't see why you did that! It makes no sense. Why go out of your way to visit the person who has made life hard for you the last few years?"

Tasha glanced at her sister, who failed to keep a smile off of her face.

"That one's all yours."

Their mother looked back and forth between the two of them.

"What's that supposed to mean? The two of you are ganging up on me," Helene said before she smiled as well. "Does that mean you're getting along now?"

"I believe we are, no thanks to you and your meddling ways," said Sara.

"I'm not meddling." Helene crossed her arms over her chest. "I'm merely assisting the two of you in getting your lives on track. Now that Tasha and Greg are together—"

"We are a long way from together, Mother. We haven't even had an official date."

Ignoring the interruption, Helene said, "Now that Tasha has a someone, I can focus on Sara. Any thoughts?"

A look of horror crossed Sara's face.

"I am not going to speed dating. Don't get any brilliant ideas. I'll figure things out on my own."

"If I wait for you to find someone, I'll never have any more grandchildren. Didn't you say you knew someone from your yoga class? Why don't you give him a call?"

The panicked expression on Sara's face as she glanced toward the kitchen had Tasha jumping in to help her sister.

"She can find her own date, Mom. Don't worry about her." Pushing back from the table, Tasha said, "Why don't we go to the living room? It'll be more comfortable."

As they moved from one room to the next, Tasha couldn't help feeling proud. Between Sunshine and her own new-found compulsion for neatness, the living room sparkled. A stack of magazines rested on the coffee table. The couch pillows were fluffed and neatly arranged. A small basket holding Blake's toys and Libby's books sat in the corner of the room. Fresh flowers brightened up the room from the vase on the entry table.

"You want to show off your clean house, don't you?" Helene asked, gliding a finger across the coffee table. It used to bother

her when her mother checked for dust. Now, she was confident her house was the best it could be. Just like herself and her family. Tasha sank into the chair and beckoned Sara and Helene to take the couch.

"Why wouldn't I want to brag a little bit?" She put her hands behind her head. "It's taken me a while to get to this point. So yeah, I'm going to show off."

"Well that's fine, but you can't distract me. I still think your sister needs to find someone."

"Who is Sara looking for?" Max asked as he joined the group in the living room. Brad and Carlton followed him. "I thought you were talking about Tasha's dating life."

The panic returned to Sara's face, and Tasha decided to change the subject completely. She picked up a large white box from the coffee table.

"Okay everyone. Listen up. Tonight was a celebration for Libby, but I also have good news." She lifted the lid off the box and the smell of chocolate filled the air. "My new housecleaner Sunshine gave me these candies."

As Tasha passed around the box, Helene asked, "Is that the woman in the bright yellow shirt I saw a while back?" Her mother handed Max a chocolate, pulled a second one for herself and then handed the box to Sara. When Tasha nodded, Helene asked, "Why would she do that?"

"Mother, can't you enjoy someone's generosity for once?" asked Sara. She held a square candy with nuts on top. "The woman is providing your dessert for Pete's sake."

Brad and Carlton each took a toffee from the box.

"Please tell her thank you," said Carlton. "This is my favorite brand of candy."

Brad nodded. "And it's nice of you to share with all of us. I have to admit, though, I had the same question as Helene."

"If everyone has their chocolate, I'll tell you." Tasha took the box from Brad and selected her treat. She waited until she had everyone's attention then raised her chocolate in the air. "I'd like to make a toast." Despite their confusion, everyone lifted their treats before she continued. "You are looking at Sunshine's most improved client! She said she's never seen someone's house turn around this fast. Sunshine wanted me to celebrate my accomplishment. It's weird that someone you just met can have an impact on you, but as you can see, my home is better because of her help."

"That's lovely, dear," said Helene. "Don't you think the housecleaner has figured out how much easier her job will be? Maybe you should consider the chocolates as a bribe. To keep it up?"

Tasha ignored her mother's cynicism. Some things would never change and her mother fit in that category. But as she learned with Doug, she could move on and take control of her life.

And I'm going to, she thought.

"Thank you. You've all helped me in some way this last couple of weeks. It has been amazing to know each of you cares for me and the kids. I've known some of you forever and others only a short time, but I couldn't have done it without you." Tasha stood up. "Here's to my best mistake. It changed my life forever."

FREE PREVIEW OF MY BEST DECISION - SARA'S STORY

I f you enjoyed My Best Mistake - Tasha's story, check out My Best Decision - Sara's Story. You can download the first three chapters for free by joining Carole's mailing list at www.carolewolfe.com.

ABOUT THE AUTHOR

Carole Wolfe started telling stories in the third grade and hasn't stopped since. While she no longer illustrates her stories with crayon, Carole still uses her words to help readers escape the daily hiccups of life.

When Carole isn't writing, she is a stay-at-home mom to three busy kiddos, a traveling husband and a dog who thinks she is a cat. Carole enjoys running at a leisurely pace, crocheting baby blankets for charity and drinking wine when she can find the time. She and her family live in Arizona.

Follow Carole's work at www.carolewolfe.com.